PRAISE FOR THE NOVELS OF
#1 NEW YORK TIMES BESTSELLING AUTHOR
BARBARA FREETHY

"I love *The Callaways*! H
suspense and sexy alpha h   .t?"
                                                    ...uthor **Bella Andre**

"I adore *The Callaways*, a family we'd all love to have. Each new book is a deft combination of emotion, suspense and family dynamics. A remarkable, compelling series!"
-- *USA Today Bestselling Author* **Barbara O'Neal**

"Once I start reading a Callaway novel, I can't put it down. Fast-paced action, a poignant love story and a tantalizing mystery in every book!"
-- *USA Today Bestselling Author* **Christie Ridgway**

"*BETWEEN NOW AND FOREVER* is a beautifully written story. Fans of Barbara's Angel's Bay series will be happy to know the search leads them to Angel's Bay where we get to check in with some old friends."
-- *The Book Momster Blog*

"A very touching story that shows the power of love and how much it can heal."
--*All Night Books for BETWEEN NOW AND FOREVER*

"In the tradition of LaVyrle Spencer, gifted author Barbara Freethy creates an irresistible tale of family secrets, riveting adventure and heart-touching romance."
-- *NYT Bestselling Author* **Susan Wiggs**
on Summer Secrets

Also By Barbara Freethy

To Anne and Poppy, my Starbucks writing pals, who are always happy to share my book journey!

BEFORE I DO

Bachelors & Bridesmaids (#4)

—➤➤◀◀—

BARBARA FREETHY

Printed in the United States of America

Cover design by Damonza.com
Interior design by Lisa Rogers lbrpub@gmail.com

ISBN: 9780996117128

One

"He's out of his mind." Nicholas Hunter stared in bewilderment at the contract in his hand. "What kind of loophole is this?"

Martin Hennessey sat back in his chair at the long table in the executive conference room of Hunter Resorts International and gave a shrug. "I'd say it's an intriguing one."

"What the hell does it mean?"

"He's got you, Nick. Face facts. Juan Carlos will not sell you his piece of prime Argentine coastline unless he gets what he wants."

"What he wants?" Nick echoed. "The man wants me to dance the tango, or am I misreading this?"

Martin grinned. "You're not misreading anything."

"He's crazy. I'm not going to do that."

"Why not? It's just a dance."

Nick tossed the contract down on the table. "What the hell happened, Martin? When I left Buenos Aires, a mere forty-eight hours ago, everything was set. You and Juan Carlos were just going to sit down and iron out the last few details."

"Juan didn't like the way you acted when you were down there. You didn't socialize with anyone. You didn't reach out to the locals. You stayed in your room or in Juan's office studying geographic maps and architectural plans."

"That's my job."

"Yes, but Juan is worried that you don't understand his country well enough to build a resort that will fit in with the natural beauty of the land, enhance the flavor, the uniqueness of Argentina—his words, not mine. He says he's a patriot first and a businessman second."

Nick paced restlessly around the room, which was part of a spacious office suite on the top floor of the Grand View Towers Hotel in downtown San Francisco. While his company operated hotels all around the world, San Francisco was his home base.

Pausing in front of the floor-to-ceiling windows, he looked down at the city. The narrow, steep streets of Nob Hill, Chinatown and North Beach filled his view, and those streets were teeming with people on a windy but clear Wednesday afternoon. Off in the distance were sailboats bobbing in the bay and the sweeping span of the Golden Gate Bridge. The view was spectacular by anyone's standards but it wasn't as good as the view in his mind.

Instead of seeing a busy city, he saw a deserted quiet beach in Argentina. The sea was turquoise and clear as crystal. The white sand stretched for miles, and the sunsets were an unbelievable mix of orange, pink and purple. He would take that strip of coastline and turn it into a world-class resort. He'd been building that hotel in his mind for fourteen years. It was past time to make it happen.

He reached into his pocket, his fingers curling around the frayed edges of the magazine photograph he couldn't seem to throw away. His long-time dream was about to come true, and he couldn't let anything get in the way. He had to find a way to buy Juan's land.

"It's just a dance," Martin said again, bringing his

attention back to the present.

He turned to face his vice president of operations. "Juan thinks if I dance the tango, I'll understand his country?"

"Yes. He's an emotional old man. The last day we were there he took me for a walk on the beach and told me about the first time his feet had touched that sand, the day he'd taken his fiancé there to propose as the sun was going down. He doesn't want to sell the land at all, but he needs the money, and he knows the local economy would benefit from having a resort there."

"Which is why he has to sell to us. He won't get a better offer."

"And you won't get him to budge on the tango. So suck it up, boss." Martin pushed a brochure across the table. "There's a dance studio not far from here. I already made a call. They teach the Argentinian tango, and they have private lessons available."

"You already made a call?"

"That's why you pay me the big bucks," Martin joked.

While Martin was his second in command, they'd also been friends for a decade, and Martin was one of the few people Nick was close to. Most everyone else he kept a good arm's length away.

"This could be good for you, Nick," Martin continued. "You've been working non-stop for the last ten years—days, nights and weekends. And forget about vacations—they don't exist in your world. Maybe it's time to take a break, catch your breath, look around and see if you've missed anything in your obsessive drive to build an empire."

"That obsessive drive is what pays your exorbitant salary," he reminded him.

"Yeah, and ordinarily I wouldn't say anything, but sometimes I worry about you."

"Nothing to worry about. Everything is going according

to plan." Or it had been until Juan Carlos had thrown a wrench in the works.

"You have just over a week to learn the dance. Juan is throwing a party a week from Sunday. He's invited us to come. You'll dance the tango. He'll sign the contract."

"Don't I need a partner?"

"Juan said he'd find you a partner if you don't have one. What about Karen? She had some nice moves."

He nodded. "Very nice and all very calculated to further her modeling career."

Martin frowned. "Someday you're going to have to tell me what went on there."

"That won't be today." He paused, another thought coming into his head. "Why don't you have to dance, Martin? Why am I the only one on the spot?"

"Because I'm not in charge," Martin replied as he got to his feet. "When you go to the dance studio, ask for the owner, Isabella Martinez. She's the tango teacher, and she got great reviews online."

"I still haven't said I'm going to do it."

"You'll do it. There isn't anything you wouldn't do for that land. We both know that."

He really hated it when Martin was right.

As Martin left the conference room, Nick picked up the dance studio brochure. On the front was a picture of an exotically beautiful dark-eyed brunette, whose inviting smile actually made him want to open the brochure.

He skimmed the list of classes, his gaze settling on two important words—private lessons. If he was going to learn to dance, he would prefer not to do it in front of an audience. He was good at a lot of things, but dancing was not even close to the top of that list.

Isabella Martinez tapped her foot restlessly against the hardwood floor. The beat of the music flowed through her soul, and she yearned to move into dance and feel the freedom of expression that was so much a part of her. But this was not her time to dance; rather, to teach.

Three couples danced in front of her, each stumbling through their own variation of the waltz. She winced as one of the women set her spiked heel down hard on her partner's foot. The man groaned, but to his credit he kept going. That wasn't completely surprising. Those two were newlyweds, and he was obviously still trying to make his new wife happy.

The other couples were both older. One was a long-married pair who had signed up for the classes so they could find something they could do together. The third couple was made up of two divorcées who had met at a singles event a few weeks earlier and discovered they shared a love of dancing. They were probably the happiest people in the room, their waltz being used as foreplay for what would come later.

Isabella looked away from her students as she was joined at the front of the room by one of the other dance instructors, Ricardo Domingo. Ricardo was tall, dark and handsome, the epitome of a Latin lover, and he was happy to play up that role, especially with the female students.

"They're not exactly Astaire and Rogers, are they?" Ricardo muttered.

"They're trying. That's what matters. One-two-three, one-two-three," she called out encouragingly. "Listen to the music, let it be your guide."

"There's a man out front who needs to speak to you," Ricardo said.

"Can't you help him?"

"He insists on talking to you. He looks like an unwilling student. You know the type."

"All too well," she said with a sigh. The male gender

usually came to her studio under some sort of duress.

"Here's his card. I'll take over for you until you get back."

Isabella looked down at the foil-embossed business card. "Nicholas Hunter, President, HRI, Hunter Resorts International. Sounds impressive, but I've never heard of him."

"That's because you spend all your time in this studio. Nicholas Hunter is a very successful businessman. He builds hotels all over the world."

"And he wants to learn how to dance?"

"Let's hope so. He can definitely pay top dollar."

"Okay. I'll be back as soon as I can."

Isabella took a quick glance in the mirror before leaving the studio. An off-the-shoulder white sweater covered her rose-colored tank top, and a filmy, flowing skirt dropped from her waist to below her knees. A pair of heels added two inches to her five-foot four-inch frame. Her face was still flushed from the demonstration she'd performed a few moments earlier and strands of long, dark brown hair fell out of her French braid. She tucked a few strands behind her ear, then went out to the lobby.

Nicholas Hunter stood in front of the glass case displaying dance trophies and photographs from various performances. Dressed in a black suit with a white button-down shirt and plum-colored silk tie, he appeared to be a successful business executive. His dark brown hair just touched the collar of his shirt, and his profile was strong and defined. When he turned to face her, his light blue eyes lit up an otherwise somber expression. She had a feeling that if he smiled, he'd take her breath away. As it was, he'd already given her pulse an unexpected jolt.

"Isabella Martinez?" he asked in a deep, husky voice.

"Yes."

"Nicholas Hunter." He shook her hand, his grip strong

and firm, which boded well for him being a good dance partner. He was a man who obviously knew how to lead.

"What can I do for you?"

"I need tango lessons."

Tango lessons? A sexy, passionate dance for this conservative businessman? "Really? Why?"

"My reasons aren't important."

"Do you have a partner?"

"No, I'm on my own."

She walked over to the counter and turned on her computer to check the class schedule. "We have a beginning tango class starting tomorrow night. Two women still need a partner. Will that work?"

"No. I want private lessons, and I need them this week. I just need one or two to learn the basics. That's it."

"You'll need more than one or two lessons to master such a complicated dance."

"I don't need to master it. I just have to be able to competently perform the dance in a little over a week."

"That's fast."

"Can you help me?"

She hesitated, wondering about his motivation. His back was stiff, his face rigid, and she couldn't imagine him dancing the tango, a raw, earthy dance that could only be done well without inhibition, without restraint. Getting this man to unbend would be a challenge.

However, she'd always loved a challenge. And she needed money, so why hadn't she already said yes?

"Of course," she said quickly.

"When can we begin?"

"Tomorrow evening. Why don't you come at the end of the group class so that you can see the demonstration that one of the other instructors and I will be putting on for the group. Then you'll have an idea of what the dance should look like."

"Fine. Do I need to bring anything?"

"Maybe some enthusiasm and a smile?"

"Why don't I just show up and you can charge me double for my bad attitude?" he said dryly.

"So you do know you have a bad attitude?"

"You're very direct, Ms. Martinez."

"Please call me Isabella, and you didn't answer the question."

"Do you need a deposit for the lessons?"

"You can pay me when you come," she said, realizing she wasn't going to get more out of him now. "I'm sure I can trust you to do that."

His frown deepened. "You shouldn't trust anyone, but I will pay you tomorrow."

As he left, she couldn't help wondering why he needed to learn the tango, why he had such a bad attitude about it, and why he didn't think anyone should be trusted, but he was obviously not a man to confide in anyone, especially not a stranger.

But tomorrow that would change, because the tango had a way of stripping away secrets and exposing the heart.

Two

---◆◆◆◆◆---

Thursday night Nicholas Hunter stood in the back of the dance studio watching Isabella Martinez and Ricardo Domingo set the dance floor on fire. Isabella's tango was like nothing he'd ever seen before. Her black silk dress swirled around her shapely legs as she spun, kicked and dipped with a sultry abandon that made his palms sweat and his heart beat faster. She was beautiful and sexy, and every move made him wonder if she would bring that same passion to the bedroom.

Clearing his throat, he told himself to focus, to remember why he was here. He needed to learn how to dance to close a deal. That was the only thing that was important. He couldn't let himself get derailed by a sexy brunette with no ring on her finger.

That might not mean anything, though. She could have taken off the ring while dancing. Or she could be involved with the man she was dancing with, a man who seemed to have entranced all the women in the room. They really were a beautiful pair. Their dance told a story, and he felt himself watching every step with a strange fascination. He also began to realize the enormity of the task in front of him.

This was the kind of dance that Juan Carlos would expect to see when he took the floor in a few weeks. How the hell was that going to happen?

Frowning, he turned his attention away from Isabella and concentrated on Ricardo. He tried to make mental notes of the technical steps involved in the dance, but they moved so quickly that was impossible. Ricardo also brought a dramatic flair, an intensity of expression to his confident steps.

For a split second, Nick was tempted to walk—make that run—to the nearest exit. But he wasn't a coward, and he hadn't run away from anything in a very long time.

The dance finally came to an end with a distinctive flourish. The class burst into applause.

As Isabella and Ricardo went over some important instructions for the couples to work on before the next class, Nick walked out to the hall and got a drink from the fountain. The cold water took down the heat in his body, and by the time he went back into the now empty studio, his heart was beating at a normal rate.

He could do this. He could learn how to dance. Maybe he wouldn't be half as good as Isabella and Ricardo, but hopefully he wouldn't completely embarrass himself.

Unfortunately, his pulse leapt again when Isabella came forward with a warm smile.

God, she was pretty with her dark eyes and sweet pink lips. There was an energy about her that enveloped him. He should have picked an older teacher, someone plainer, someone who wouldn't be distracting or challenging. But it was too late now.

"What did you think?" she asked.

"It was—nice."

She raised an eyebrow. "Nice? Surely it was better than nice?"

"It was very good," he amended. "You and your partner are incredibly talented."

"Thank you. I know it can be a little overwhelming at the beginning, but you don't need to worry. I'm as good a teacher as I am a dancer."

Her charming confidence didn't really make him feel better, because it only made her more appealing, and the last thing he needed to complicate his life right now was a woman. But all he said was, "I'm counting on that. So how do we start?"

"Let me put the music back on."

"Really? Music already?" he asked as she moved across the room. "Don't I need to learn the steps first?"

"You will. I want you to listen closely to the beat, the rhythm," she said as she turned on the music.

He stood self-consciously in the middle of the studio feeling like a fool as he saw himself in the mirror. He'd come straight from work and his white shirt, dark blue tie, black tie and expensive Italian shoes didn't make him look much like a dancer. But he wasn't a dancer. He was an entrepreneur, a businessman, and this was just another part of his job.

"I promise this won't hurt a bit," Isabella said as she rejoined him.

"That's what my dentist says before he jabs me with a long needle."

She extended her hands, palms open. "I'm unarmed."

He didn't think her weapons were her hands. It was her smile and eyes that could probably kill him.

"Let me show you some of the basic positions." She took his hands and placed one around her waist and then stretched the other out to the side. "Are you comfortable?"

"It's all right. Now what?"

"Now, we do the first simple combination of steps and we count."

She showed him how to do the first five steps. He stumbled through her count that began with a one-two-three, and ended with an "ouch" as he stepped on her foot.

"Sorry," he said. "I knew this would be painful."

"Apparently for both of us," she agreed. "Let's try it again. If it's at all possible for you to lose some of the stiffness, that would be awesome."

He had no idea how to lose the stiffness. He'd acquired a hard shell climbing up the corporate ladder, and he rarely let down his guard. He forced himself to try to relax as they went through the steps again.

"Better," she said. "Now you're going to lead me across the room. I want us to glide—effortlessly. Then we will make a sharp turn and ended on a pointed step. Got it?"

He seriously doubted it he was even close to getting it. "Let's give it a shot," he said tersely.

"Hold on."

"What?"

"There's something you need to understand, Mr. Hunter. Actually, may I call you Nicholas?"

"Nick works. And what is it that I need to understand?"

"The tango is a dance of passion, excitement. Every movement is designed to entice, seduce. It's a push-pull battle of desire—need warring with resistance." She took his hand and twirled her body into his, coming to a stop with her hands on his chest, the tip of her head just touching his chin.

His pulse quickened beneath her palms. He wanted to put his arms around her. He wanted to pull her even closer and cover her mouth with his. Before he could act on any of those thoughts, she pushed off, spinning away from him.

"See what I mean?" she asked. "We come together, then break apart. The dance is a seduction, and if done correctly, the audience will yearn to see the dancers come together, to surrender to their desires."

Every one of her words raised the heat level in his body. He swallowed a growing knot in his throat and let go of her hand. "I don't think this is going to work."

She gave him a surprised look. "We've just gotten

started."

"I'm not a dancer."

"You will be when we're done. You have to give yourself a chance."

"This is more complicated than I thought."

"Yes, it is, but that's what makes the tango so special."

He wasn't just talking about the dance; he was talking about her, but she didn't need to know that.

She gave him a speculative look. "I wouldn't have thought you'd quit so easily."

He frowned. He'd never been a quitter, but he had excellent self-preservation instincts, and everything about Isabella and this damn dance was telling him to run.

"It's really not that difficult," she continued. "I'm sure you've seduced a woman or two or three."

"Not with dancing," he muttered.

"So you'll have something new to add to your game," she said with a smile. "Maybe this would be easier for you if you brought your own partner. Do you have a woman in your life you'd feel more comfortable dancing with?"

"No," he said shortly.

"Then what do you want to do?"

He hesitated. "Let's keep going."

"Good." She extended her hand, and he took it.

For the next twenty minutes, he followed her patient instructions and managed to learn a few combinations before Isabella called a halt.

"That's enough for tonight," she said.

"Thank God." He ran the back of his hand across his sweaty brow.

She laughed. "There's a patio outside. Care for some air?"

"Sounds great." He followed her out the side door and found himself on a small patio surrounded by tall buildings.

The night was clear of San Francisco's usual fog bank and the mid-May weather was unusually warm.

"It's a nice night," Isabella said, taking a seat at the table. "It feels like summer is not too far away."

He sat down across from her. "Summer in San Francisco isn't always that warm."

She tipped her head in agreement. "Very true. Are you a native?"

"I am. What about you?"

"I was born in Buenos Aires."

His gut tightened at her words. "I didn't realize that."

"Why would you? It's not on my studio brochure."

"When did you come to the States?"

"When I was eight." A shadow filled her eyes. "My parents got divorced, and my mother brought me to San Francisco."

"Was your mother American?"

"Yes. She was a translator working for the Foreign Service when she met my father at the U.S. Embassy in Argentina. He was a lawyer. They had a whirlwind romance and married within six months of meeting each other. But their love affair was too hot to last long."

"Sorry."

She shrugged. "It is what it is. I don't remember them being happy together, so I can't say I miss those times."

"What about your father? Is he still in Argentina?"

"He is," she said, a sad note in her voice. "He's been out of my life for a very long time."

"You didn't see him after the divorce?" he asked, wondering why he was so curious. He usually avoided getting personal, because once a woman answered questions about herself, she usually had questions for him.

"I saw my father twice after the divorce. I remember each one in vivid detail. The first was my ninth birthday. We didn't make it to the cake before he and my mom got into a fight and she told him to get out. The next time was my eighth-grade graduation. He gave me a bouquet of flowers and told me he wanted me to come and see him and my grandparents in Argentina that summer. He was going to convince my mother it would be a good idea." A sad gleam entered her eyes. "But he couldn't convince her. She wouldn't let me go. She was very stubborn about it. I never saw him again after that. That was thirteen years ago."

"There was no contact between the two of you after that?"

"There were some letters, emails, a couple of texts, and then nothing." She paused, her gaze reflective. "I used to think about going to Argentina to see him, to ask him why he'd abandoned me. But I could never quite get to the point of buying an actual ticket. My mother didn't want me to have any contact with him, so she was also somewhat of an obstacle."

"Did she explain why she didn't want you to have a relationship?"

"She said he had a lot of problems, and she didn't want his problems to become mine."

"What kind of problems?"

"She was never specific, but I think he had a problem with alcohol. I know that they used to argue about his drinking. I occasionally tried to press for more information, but it always upset her, so I stopped. My mom had to work hard to support us. I don't know if my dad ever gave her any money. Maybe he did, but our lifestyle was very modest. We lived in the same apartment building as my mother's sister, and my Aunt Rhea became my second mom. She's the reason I became a dancer. She opened this dance studio when I was eleven, and I would come here after school. Whenever I was anxious or frazzled, I would dance."

"And that made you feel better?" he asked doubtfully.

She smiled. "Yes, it did. Dance is a great stress reliever. My aunt studied ballet from the time she was three, and she was amazingly disciplined. When she started to teach me, she would work me out until I was dripping with sweat and every muscle in my body was aching. But it was a good ache, the kind that comes from hard work and a sense of achievement. When I was upset about my father or my life, Aunt Rhea would take me to the ballet barre. She would put my hands on the barre and say, 'This is home. This is where your center is. When you're spinning out of control, you come here. You remember what's important.' It always worked." She cleared her throat. "I'm rambling. Sorry."

"Don't apologize. I've never met a dancer before. It's interesting. Did you ever dance professionally?"

She stiffened at his question, and it was the first time since they'd met that she seemed uncomfortable. "I did, yes."

"Where?"

"New York, L.A., London."

"That sounds impressive."

"I had some good things going for a while, but I got injured, and everything went bad."

"You couldn't go back to the barre and get it back?"

She sighed. "I tried, but time had moved on, and I needed to come up with a new plan. So I decided to teach, help my aunt run the studio."

"And you don't miss performing?"

"Sometimes I do, but teaching others can be fulfilling, too." She took a breath. "Let's talk about you."

There it was—the personal questions in reverse. He should have known better. "My life has not been as interesting as yours."

"I seriously doubt that. Tell me why you want to learn to dance the tango."

"It's a requirement for a business deal."

She raised an eyebrow in surprise. "That's the first time I've ever heard that answer. What's the deal?"

He didn't usually like to share business details, but he might need her help. In fact, he knew he was going to need her help, because the one thing he'd learned from his first lesson was that if he was going to successfully dance the tango, he would need a good teacher and a good partner.

"I want to buy a piece of land in Argentina. The owner of the land wants to make sure that I understand his country and his culture. Apparently, my dancing the tango for him will prove that."

"It might help," she agreed. "I don't know anything about your deal, but I do know that the tango is part of the Argentinian culture. If you can understand the passion behind the dance, you'll have a better understanding of the people who dance it. And if nothing else, you'll have learned something new in life. Nothing wrong with that."

"I prefer to learn new things that can help me in my business."

"Well, apparently the tango is going to help you in your business."

"True," he conceded. "If I can find a way not to trip over my feet."

"You will. You just have to learn how to get out of your own way."

"You're making it sound easier than it will be. You and Ricardo were amazing partners. I can't imagine getting to that point."

"Ricardo and I have known each other for years. He first came to the studio when he was fifteen, and I was thirteen. We grew up together. We know each other's strengths and weaknesses. That's why we tango so well. But each pair of tango dancers is different. When you and I dance..." Her voice drifted away.

"What?" he pressed. "What happens when you and I dance?"

She looked him straight in the eye. "I'm not sure yet. We're just getting to know each other."

That was true. As much as he didn't want to dance, he found himself wanting to get to know her better. She was one of the most interesting women he'd spoken to in a very long time. But he hadn't come here to find a date. He needed to stay focused. "When can we meet again? Tomorrow night?"

She hesitated. "Friday night? You don't have other plans?"

"I will make myself available for these lessons. I don't have much time before I have to perform the dance."

"Tomorrow night might work. I'll have to check my schedule."

She'd no sooner finished speaking than the studio door opened and a slender, dark-haired, dark-eyed woman walked out to the patio. She appeared to be in her late forties, early fifties and bore a striking resemblance to Isabella.

"Aunt Rhea," Isabella said in surprise. "When did you get back from L.A.?"

"About fifteen minutes ago," Rhea answered, giving Nick a curious look. "Hello."

"This is Nicholas Hunter," Isabella quickly said. "My aunt, Rhea Carvello."

"Nice to meet you," he said, getting up to shake Rhea's hand.

"You, too. I didn't mean to interrupt."

"I just finished giving Nick a tango lesson," Isabella said.

"Out here?" Rhea challenged with a curious smile.

"No, we were getting some air. The studio was quite warm tonight. I don't think the fan is working that well."

"Or maybe the tango got you all hot and bothered," Rhea

said with a gleam in her eyes. "At any rate, I just came by to tell you that I have some news. It may not make you happy, but I think I have to consider it."

"You're not talking about selling the studio again?" Isabella asked, tension in her voice.

"I have an offer, Isabella. It's a good one. I want you to look at it with me."

"I don't want you to sell. So, no thanks."

"Oh, honey, I know it will be a big change, but I need to move on."

"And I understand that, but I want to be the one who buys the studio from you. I'm working on a plan to make that happen."

"We both know a buyout will take more money than you have."

"Business has been increasing," Isabella argued. "And I have some other ideas, too."

Rhea frowned. "I don't want to make you unhappy, Isabella, but I don't want to worry about this studio anymore. I've given up a lot for this place and now it's my turn. David and I have something special. We want to travel. We want to be free of debt and responsibility."

"I understand, but just give me some time," she pleaded.

"All right, we'll talk again later." Rhea paused. "I'm sorry, Nick. I interrupted your session with my personal business."

"Not a problem." He stood up. "I should be going anyway."

"I'll walk you out," Isabella said as she rose. "We can check the schedule on the way out and see how tomorrow night works."

They walked back into the studio together.

Rhea said goodbye in the lobby, leaving them alone by the front counter.

"So your aunt wants to sell this place?" he asked.

Isabella opened her calendar on the computer and nodded, a grim expression on her face. "Yes. She fell in love last year with a man who lives in Los Angeles. He wants her to move down there and live with him. I can't blame her for wanting to do that. She's been single forever, and now she wants to have a relationship. I just don't want her to sell the studio to a stranger. It means everything to me."

"It's your home." He remembered the passion and emotion in her earlier words.

"Exactly. She taught me to love this studio, and now she wants to sell it and have me be happy about it."

"It sounds like she wants to be happy herself."

"I know, and I'm trying to put her interests in front of mine, because she's done a lot for me, but it's not easy."

"Let me ask you another question. Is the studio profitable?"

She sighed. "I'm sure the answer would be no by most standards. But this place isn't just about money; it's about dreams."

He smiled. "You're talking like a dancer, not a business owner. Everything is about money. It makes the world go round."

She frowned at him. "I don't agree. The arts are an important part of a civilized society."

"But you can't continue to teach that art if you don't make money. From what your aunt said, it sounds like she's been struggling to keep this place afloat for a long time."

"Business is better now," she argued. "I'm not going to let this studio go without a fight."

He appreciated the light of battle in her eyes. Too many people gave up too easily; Isabella obviously wasn't one of them.

"So tomorrow night," she said, looking down at the

computer. "I can do eight o'clock. Will that work?"

As much as he wanted to say no, he knew he had to say yes. The clock was ticking. "I'll see you then."

Three

---→ ❯❯ ❮❮ ←---

"Isabella, Isabella? Are you there?" Liz Palmer snapped her fingers in front of Isabella's face.

"Sorry," she said, realizing she'd drifted away in the middle of lunch on Friday with two of her good friends, Liz Palmer and Julie Michaels. They'd met a half hour earlier at the Delano Street Café by San Francisco's Embarcadero, and judging by the curious expressions in both sets of eyes, she'd been distracted for far too long. "What did you ask me?"

"What's going on with you?" Liz said. "It's like you're in a daze."

"I have a lot on my mind," she replied.

"The studio?" Julie asked sympathetically.

She'd told Julie about her aunt's plans to sell the studio the night before when they'd confirmed lunch. "That and…" She stopped, realizing that a good part of her distraction was not just about the studio but also about Nicholas Hunter.

"And?" Liz prodded. "There's a guy, isn't there?"

She frowned. "It doesn't always have to be a guy."

"But it is, right?"

"I did get a new student last night," she admitted. "He's very interesting."

"As in sexy, single, take-to-bed kind of interesting?"

Julie enquired.

"I think he's single, and he's very attractive, off-the-charts sex appeal, but...he's also a very controlled person. He doesn't smile much. He's very reserved with his conversation. So he's not really my type. I prefer more outgoing men. But he does have thick, wavy dark brown hair, a killer body, and a pair of light blue eyes that are amazingly intense."

Julie laughed. "He definitely made an impression on you. No wonder you're daydreaming."

"What kind of lessons is he taking?" Liz asked. "I hope he's not getting ready for his wedding. That's when most men seem to want to learn how to dance."

"No, he's not doing that. He wants to learn the tango. It's part of some sort of business deal."

"That's an unusual deal," Liz commented. "What's this guy's name?"

"His name is Nicholas Hunter, and he's the president and founder of Hunter Resorts International."

Liz's jaw dropped. "I know who Nicholas Hunter is. Several years ago I worked on a promotional campaign for the Grand View Towers."

"Really?" she said in surprise.

"I have to admit I didn't have any meetings with him personally, but his company was wonderful to work with. A year later, his assistant sent me a complimentary stay at his Hawaii hotel, which was awesome." Liz paused, a glitter of excitement in her eyes. "I did happen to see Nick Hunter walk by the conference room one day and the man is gorgeous. He's also extremely wealthy. What on earth is he doing taking dancing lessons at your studio?"

"I told you—it's part of some business deal."

"That must be some deal."

"I didn't get the details. I'm a teacher. He wants lessons. I wasn't going to say no."

"Maybe you could be more than student and teacher," Liz suggested with a sparkling smile. "I'm pretty sure he's single."

"I was thinking the same thing," Julie put in. "Especially now that I've just heard Liz rave about him. She's usually extremely picky and judgmental about men."

Liz rolled her eyes but didn't deny Julie's good-natured comment.

Isabella smiled fondly at her friends. "Ever since you two fell in love and got engaged, you've been trying to set me up with every single guy who crosses my path. You need to stop. I'm not desperate, and I'm not that eager to get involved with anyone. I have a lot of other things to worry about right now. If you want to help me brainstorm something, help me figure out how to buy my aunt's studio without having enough money."

"What about your mom?" Liz suggested. "Could she help?"

She shook her head. "My mother has finally gotten to a place in her life where she doesn't have to work two jobs. I can't ask her for money."

"Maybe Matt and I could invest," Julie offered. "Matt has made a lot of money the past few years."

As the star baseball player for the Cougars, Isabella knew that was true, but she didn't want to borrow from her friends.

"So has Michael," Liz interjected. "And Andrea's husband Alex could probably help as well."

She immediately shook her head. "No, thank you. This is my problem, and I will figure it out. I appreciate the offers, but you both have weddings to plan, and Alex and Andrea have recently set up a huge foundation to support foster kids in the city. I need to figure this out without taking charity from my friends."

"It's not charity," Liz said. "It would be a loan."

"I couldn't take a loan unless I knew for sure I could pay

it back, and I honestly don't know that. So, I need to keep thinking."

"Maybe you should keep thinking about whether or not you really want to buy the studio," Julie said. "You're a dancer, Isabella. You're a performer. I know your career was derailed by your injury, but are you sure you don't want to try to get it back?"

"I don't think so," she said slowly. As much as she missed performing, she didn't miss the pain and disappointment and frustration of the last two years. "Enough about me. Let's talk about your wedding, Liz. I can't believe it's only three weeks away. How are all the plans coming along? Do you need my help with anything?"

"It's all good," Liz replied. "Maggie is taking care of everything at the Stratton. And the hotel gardens are already blooming, so it's going to be beautiful. My dad's health has improved, so he'll be able to walk me down the aisle."

"That's wonderful news," she said, seeing the moisture in Liz's eyes. Her father had been battling cancer for a couple of years and it had been touch-and-go the last few months. Apparently things were better now.

"It means a lot to me to have my dad give me away," Liz said, dabbing at her eyes with her napkin. "I can't believe I'm crying. I'm so *not* a crier."

"Weddings bring it out in all of us," Julie said, blinking some suspicious brightness out of her eyes.

"What's just as important as having my dad with me," Liz continued, "is having my friends by my side. I'm thrilled that everyone is going to make it—even Jessica."

"We made a pact," Isabella said with a smile. "And you were nice enough to schedule your wedding when school gets out so Jessica could make it."

"That is partly why I picked June, so I'm glad it worked out for everyone. I have to admit I had no idea planning a wedding could be so time-consuming and stressful. I've been trying to convince Julie that she and Matt should just get married at the same time so she could avoid all this craziness."

"I would," Julie said with a laugh, "but Matt can't get married in the middle of baseball season. We're shooting for next November or maybe Christmas, but definitely after the World Series, just in case the Cougars go all the way."

"The way Matt is swinging a bat lately, along with the rest of the Cougars, I'd say the World Series is a definite possibility," Liz said. "But it would have been fun to have a double wedding."

"It will be even better for you to have your own day," Julie replied. "But that does mean you're all going to have to buy another bridesmaid's dress when Matt and I tie the knot."

Isabella grinned. With two weddings done and Liz's upcoming nuptials, she already had three bridesmaid's dresses in her closet. Thankfully, her friends had pretty good taste so she'd be able to wear some of them again.

"I can't believe I'm going to be someone's wife," Liz murmured, with a bewildered shake of her head. "I thought I'd be the last of us to get married."

"Michael has had his eye on you since high school," Julie reminded Liz. "And you were just as enamored with him. You both just had to get over being competitors so you could be lovers."

"Very true," Liz agreed.

Isabella shook her head as Liz and Julie exchanged happy glances. "While I love seeing both of you in love, I think I'm going to have to start hanging out with the single women in our group before I start feeling like a complete loser."

"You're not a loser, you're just picky," Julie said.

"And I have a better idea for you," Liz put in. "Give

Nicholas Hunter a chance to be more than a student."

"I don't think that's a wise idea. That man has heartbreaker written all over him."

"Since when have you been afraid to throw yourself in the air and hope someone will catch you?" Liz challenged. "You've always been the one willing to jump first, ask questions later."

"Is it because of what happened with Carter?" Julie ventured warily, as if unsure how Isabella would react to the mention of her last boyfriend and their painful breakup.

"I don't know. Maybe. But I'm not really focused on having a relationship right now. I have more important things to worry about than finding a man. I need to figure out how to buy my aunt's studio without borrowing money from my friends."

"Maybe some targeted fundraisers would bring in some cash," Julie suggested, her expertise in non-profit fundraising making her the perfect person to suggest that option

"Or an outreach to dance patrons," Liz put in, using her P.R. skills. "There must be some wealthy people who would like to support a studio of dancers. You have to figure out what to offer them in return."

"Okay, let's keep going," she said, happy to have two smart women to help her figure things out.

—➤➤◄◄—

Isabella walked into her studio after lunch with a few new ideas spinning around her head, thanks to Liz and Julie. While most of the fundraisers seemed like long shots, they might bring in enough cash to at least make a down payment. Perhaps her aunt would let her pay the rest over time. Feeling more optimistic, she put her bag into the drawer behind the counter and checked the computer for any urgent emails.

"Isabella, thank God you're here," Ricardo said bursting through the hallway door with panic in his eyes. "Why didn't you answer my texts?"

"My phone was off. I just got back. What's wrong?"

"A water pipe burst in the ceiling. By the time we got the main valve shut off, both studios were flooded."

"Tell me you're kidding," she breathed.

"I wish I were. This is an old building. Your aunt has been holding things together with duct tape and a prayer the last ten years. You know that."

She knew money had always been tight but not that there were problems with the building itself. "It will be fine. We'll clean up, dry things off." She started to move past him so she could see the damage, but he blocked her way.

"It's not going to be that easy. The hardwood floors are damaged. They'll need to be completely redone. Jenny is in the back office calling all of our students. We'll have to cancel for at least a week or two, possibly more."

"Maybe it won't take that long."

"It's going to take time just to find contractors to do the work. I called Rhea. She'll be here in thirty minutes."

Great. Her aunt would no doubt see this latest disaster as a reason to sell out quickly as possible, although maybe the buyer would have second thoughts if he saw the damage. She hated to think that way, but she was trying to find a silver lining. "Let me take a look."

She walked down the hallway and into the main studio, staring in horror at the dripping walls and deep puddles of water that two of her staff members were trying to mop up with towels. It was worse than she'd expected.

"It's not just the floors we have to worry about; it's also the plumbing," Ricardo added. "Obviously, the pipes will have to be replaced. The showers, toilets, and sinks won't be usable until we have water again. It's not going to be an easy fix."

"We'll find a way," she said, feeling a little desperate to believe her own words.

"I don't know, Isabella. Maybe it's time for both of us to move on. Your aunt is already halfway out the door. And your injury is completely healed now. You could go back to dancing. Your career was just taking off when you got hurt."

"It's been too long. I can't go back. That part of my life is over."

"It doesn't have to be."

"I don't want to talk about the past; I need to concentrate on the present. We have insurance. That should pay for something. We'll get bids to repair everything. We'll find a way to make it work." She raised her chin in the air and gave him a determined look. "Don't quit on me, Ricardo. I need you here."

"I have bills to pay, too."

"I'm confident that I can turn things around."

He shrugged. "I won't make any decisions for a week. Longer than that, I can't promise."

"I'll take whatever I can get." She paused, her mind whirring with how to deal with the most immediate problems. While repairs were urgent, they also needed to keep the income flowing in. "Maybe we can move some of our private lessons to the homes of our students."

"Good idea. You don't have any privates until next week, do you?"

"Actually, I have one tonight—Nicholas Hunter."

"Nicholas Hunter, right," Ricardo muttered. "He lives in a mansion in Pacific Heights."

"How do you know that?"

"I looked him up last night. I was curious about him. He has a big portfolio."

"I'm not interested in his portfolio. He's just a student."

"A student with a lot of money. Maybe he'd like to make a donation to help with the repairs."

"He's taken one class. I can't ask him for money."

"Well, you're going to have to ask someone for money."

"I'd prefer that be a bank or the insurance company."

"You could mention our problems to Mr. Hunter. He might have some ideas. His father Thomas Hunter runs a venture capital firm."

"You looked up his father, too?"

"He was mentioned in the same article."

"Well, I doubt a venture capitalist would have any interest in a dance studio."

"Probably not," Ricardo agreed. "But we're desperate, and they can only say no. Just think about it."

"I'm going to think about everything, but let's take it one step at a time. Once we know what the insurance company will pay for, we'll have a better idea what kind of cash we're going to need."

"What about our classes? Are we just going to cancel?"

"We'll find another site. Maybe we can share space with another studio. Call Impulse Dance; they might be willing to share."

"All right."

"I'll make some calls tomorrow, too. It's going to work out, Ricardo. I'm not going to lose the studio."

"Well, if anyone can make a miracle happen, it's probably   you."

Four

—➤➤◄◄◄—

"She's late." Nicholas paced restlessly around the living room while Martin sat on the couch sipping a glass of wine and looking through the contracts they'd just finished signing.

"She'll be here," Martin said. "You should be happy that you didn't have to go down to the studio."

He would have actually preferred to continue his dance lessons at the studio, but that wasn't going to happen. Some plumbing crisis had apparently shut down the school, and Isabella had told him they could do it at his house or wait a few days. Since he didn't have a few days to wait, he had agreed to have her come to his house. Now, he wished he'd come up with another plan.

It wasn't that he didn't have plenty of room for a tango lesson in his two-story, five-bedroom, four-bath house, and his home was certainly private, but letting Isabella into his personal space made him uneasy. He'd already spent way too much time thinking about their conversation the night before.

She'd shared personal information with him, and he'd found himself liking her a lot. What he hadn't liked was the way she'd looked at him, like she could see into his head. He prided himself on his poker face, on not giving anything away, but she'd gotten to him with her sexy smile and those gorgeous eyes and the lips he couldn't stop thinking about tasting. He needed to keep their dance lessons professional and as short as possible.

"What's with you?" Martin asked, giving him a speculative glance. "She's not that late. It's three minutes after seven."

"Late is late. And my problem is you." He knew he sounded completely unreasonable, but he wanted to yell at someone, and Martin was unfortunately the only one around.

"Me?" Martin raised an eyebrow. "What did I do?"

"You let Juan add that amendment to the contract. You should have talked him out of it. What the hell kind of negotiator are you?"

"A damned good one, but I had no choice. It was the tango or nothing, and I didn't think you wanted nothing." Martin paused. "And if you want to blame someone, look in the mirror. You brought this on yourself by not opening up to Juan. He doesn't feel like he knows who you are."

"Well, he's not going to find out who I am by watching me dance the tango. I suck at it."

"You'll get better. I've never seen you fail to achieve a goal once you set your mind to it. You need to stop fighting the fact that you have to do this and just do it."

He frowned at Martin's good advice. "Easy for you to say. You're not going to have to take the stage."

"What are you going to do about a partner, Nick?"

"I don't know yet. Right now I'm just concentrating on my part."

"Juan did say he could provide you with a partner, so you don't have to take someone with you, but it might make you feel more comfortable to dance with someone you know."

"I doubt anything will make me feel comfortable."

The doorbell rang, and his pulse immediately jumped. He should be happy Isabella had arrived. The sooner they got started, the sooner this would be over, but he felt a strange sense of wariness as he opened the door.

Isabella wore a clingy red dress and high heels that showed off her great legs and beautiful body. Her brown hair was loose and fell around her shoulders in flowing silky waves. The smile in her dark brown eyes sent a rush of desire through his body. This was just a dance lesson he reminded himself. Nothing to get excited about.

"Sorry I'm late," she said. "I hit some unexpected construction a few blocks from here."

"They're fixing a sinkhole," he replied.

"Apparently, I share plumbing problems with the city," she said lightly. "May I come in?"

"Of course," he said, stepping aside.

As she entered the house, she paused in the marble-floored foyer, an expression of awe filling her eyes. Her gaze swept the room, obviously taking note of the sweeping staircase, the crystal chandelier and the arched doorways leading into rooms on either side of the entry. "This is beautiful," she murmured. "Have you lived here long?"

"Only a year. I can't take credit for the décor. It was professionally decorated."

"The designer did an excellent job from what I've seen so far."

"I'll give you a tour later. Why don't you come into the living room?" He ushered her through the arched doorway on the left. Martin got up from the sofa and came forward with an interested smile on his face.

"This is Martin Hennessy, my vice president of operations—Isabella Martinez, my extremely talented dance teacher."

"It's nice to meet you," Isabella said, shaking Martin's hand.

"Likewise," Martin returned. "So do you think Nick has any hope of learning the tango in the next week?"

"Absolutely," she replied.

"That sounds confident. Can I get a preview?"

"Absolutely not," Nick cut in.

"Why not? I can give you a critique."

"I have Isabella for that. I don't need anyone else. I'll see you on Monday. Have a good weekend."

"You, too." Martin grabbed his jacket off the arm of the couch. "Good luck, Isabella. I think you're going to need it."

Nick glanced at Isabella as Martin left them alone. "Are you really as confident as you sound?"

"Yes. It's just a dance, Nick. I'm not trying to teach you how to do brain surgery in a week. I think we can come up with a passable tango over the next few days."

Her words brought a reluctant smile to his lips. "Am I your worst student?"

"Not even close. That would be Jeremy Walters."

"What's wrong with Jeremy?"

"He likes to trip whoever is next to him. But then, he's ten."

"So I'm not as bad as a ten-year-old."

"No. You just need to relax and stop fighting yourself."

"Easier said than done. Do you want something to drink before we start?"

"No, I'm fine." She looked around the room. "I'm happy with the hardwood floors, but do you mind if I move some furniture around?"

"Not at all." He spent the next ten minutes pushing the couches against the wall and opening up some floor space.

"Now, the music," Isabella said. "I'm guessing you have some type of speaker system built in that I can plug my music into?"

He took the player out of her hand and popped it into the dock on the shelf. Within seconds, the room was filled with a sensual beat.

"So, do we start where we left off?" he asked.

"Actually, I just want you to listen to the music for a few moments. Don't think about it. Don't visualize steps in your head. Just let yourself feel it." She put her hand on his chest. "In here. In your heart."

He could feel the warmth of her hand through the thin dress shirt he wore, and it took a great deal of willpower not to cover her hand with his and hold her there for as long as he could. But Isabella was already moving away.

She closed her eyes, and as the strains of Latin music began to escalate, a dreamy expression came over her face. He knew he was supposed to be hearing the music, but he was more fascinated with her face, with the way her body swayed to the music in gentle seduction. He wanted to reach for her—not to dance, but to pull her close. Beads of perspiration gathered on his forehead. Damn, he was starting to sweat, and he hadn't moved one inch.

Isabella opened her eyes and looked at him. "Nick?"

There was a question in her voice, one he couldn't begin to answer.

"Are you ready to dance now?" She extended her hand.

He was more than ready to take her hand. It was just too bad a dance had to follow, but he couldn't say no to anything that got his hands on her body.

He moved into the position she'd taught him the night before. His first steps were a stumbling mess, but her patience got him over the initial hurdles. As she moved with him and against him, their legs tangled together. Her breasts brushed his chest. Her fingers tightened around his. And when the music stopped, he found himself lost in her dark brown eyes. She stared back at him, her breath coming a little too fast.

He didn't know which one of them moved first.

But suddenly he was holding her the way he wanted to, kissing her the way he'd dreamed, and she was kissing him back with the same passionate intensity she'd brought to the dance. Searing heat enveloped them. Each taste propelled him back for another and another. He wanted her closer, wanted to feel her flesh beneath his fingers, to make her feel what he was feeling—an unexpected, shocking, overwhelming wave of need.

"Wait, stop," Isabella said breathlessly, breaking away from his kiss.

He stared at her in bemusement, seeing the desire in her eyes, the softness in her lips. "Really?"

She hesitated, then nodded and took herself out of his embrace. "We can't do this. It's not good."

"I thought it was very good," he returned, feeling a chill run through him now that she'd left his arms.

"It was, but…you know what I mean. I'm you're teacher."

"So what? I'm not a kid. We're not breaking any laws."

"It's unprofessional. You hired me to do a job, and I let myself get carried away in the moment. That's a bad habit I really need to break. I'm sorry."

The last thing he wanted from her was an apology. He drew in a breath and ran a hand through his hair. "If you're apologizing, then I should do the same, but I'm not really sorry."

She licked her lips and his body tightened again.

They stared at each other for a long moment.

"I wouldn't mind having that drink you offered before," she said finally.

He could definitely use a drink. Maybe not alcohol, though. Ice water would be a better choice. "Sure," he said. "Let's go into the kitchen."

She gave him a relieved smile as they headed down the hallway. He told himself that he should be happy she'd stopped them from going any further, because now that he wasn't caught up in the damned dance, he was starting to think again.

Getting involved with Isabella would only add another complication to his life, and he didn't need that, not now, not with so much on the line. He needed her to teach him the tango. He didn't have time to start over with someone else. He just had to focus on the business part of their arrangement and nothing else.

When they entered the gourmet kitchen, he moved toward the large refrigerator and asked, "What would you like?"

"What do you have?"

"Probably anything you could want," he said as he opened the door. "My housekeeper keeps the kitchen well stocked."

Isabella came up next to him and viewed the organized shelves. "You do have everything. Impressive. I'll just take a bottled water."

"You got it." He pulled out two waters and handed her one.

She slid onto the stool at the oversized island while he leaned against the opposing counter, making sure there was a good five feet between them.

"Does your housekeeper live in?" Isabella asked.

"No, she lives with her husband a few miles from here. She works nine-to-five, give or take a few hours here and there. She manages the household staff."

"You have a staff, too?"

He shrugged. "A gardener, a cleaning service, occasionally a chef or a caterer if I'm hosting a dinner."

"You live a good life."

"I've worked hard to get it." He didn't know why he added that statement except that for some reason he didn't want Isabella to see him as someone who'd been given anything. He'd earned his way to this lifestyle, something his father had not thought he could do. And he was proud of what he'd accomplished.

"How did you get started in the hotel business?" she asked.

"That's a long story," he replied quickly. "Let's talk about your business instead. What happened at your studio today?

"A water pipe broke and damaged the studios. We had to temporarily shut down the school."

"Sounds like a mess."

She nodded. "At the worst possible time."

"Because your aunt wants to sell."

"Yes. When she saw the damage, I could see her face pale and her shoulders literally sag under the weight of this new problem. I tried to talk to her about repairs and insurance, and she just said she needed to think about what she wanted to do."

"Her buyer may withdraw his or her interest if the studio repairs are extensive."

"Which might be good for me. I will have more time to figure out a way to raise cash to buy my aunt out. On the other hand, it's going to make all of our lives more difficult, including my aunt's, and I really don't want her to be burdened when she so obviously wants out." Isabella let out a sigh. "Anyway, it's a setback. But I will find a way to make things work."

He liked that she wasn't whining or crying about her bad luck. Instead, there was a determined light in her eyes that told him she wasn't going down without a fight. "Can you find some other space to hold your classes in until your studio floors are repaired?"

"I've been looking into that." She paused, licking her lips. "Actually, I had an idea on my way over here tonight."

By the look in her eyes, he was sure he was not going to like her idea. "What's that?" he asked warily.

"You own the Grand View Towers, right? And that hotel

has a ballroom that could be divided into smaller rooms, maybe with moveable dance floors brought in?"

"I see where you're going with this. You want me to rent you some space?"

"Do you have any available?"

"I don't actually know the answer to that question. I'd have to check with the manager. The hotel ballroom is quite busy in the spring with wedding receptions."

"Which probably usually happen on the weekends," she said hopefully. "I know it's a huge thing to ask. We don't even know each other, and I'm probably way out of line, but I'm desperate. Would you consider checking to see if you have any space that we might be able to rent at a really good price?"

"Would that price be free?" he asked dryly.

"Only if you insisted," she said.

He smiled. "You're a better negotiator than I would have thought."

"It doesn't have to be free, but it would have to be cheap. What do you say?"

The idea of dance students trekking in and out of his five-star hotel was not that appealing, but he didn't want to dim the light in her eyes. It seemed cruel, which was an unusual thought for him. He was very good at keeping emotions out of his business operations. "I'll check with the manager and see what I have available. No guarantees."

"I understand. Thank you. It's not just about the money I'll be losing by shutting down the school. I hate to disappoint the students."

"You think they would be that sad to miss a few classes?"

"Most of my students really want to learn to dance, so yes. In addition to adult classes, I also teach a lot of kids, and we have a junior dance competition team that needs to practice every day."

"I didn't realize." Her business was a lot bigger than he'd thought. Actually, he hadn't given it much thought at all. He'd been focused only on what he needed to get from the school, from Isabella.

Isabella set down her empty water bottle. "Shall we get back to our lesson?"

The idea of taking her in his arms again was more than a little appealing. But he didn't want to dance with her; he wanted to go to bed with her. Being alone with her was only fueling the fire behind that desire. "I think we've done enough for now."

"We've barely done anything," she countered.

"I'll pay you for the full session."

"I'm not worried about that. I'm concerned about the time we have for you to learn this dance. Just a little over a week, right? I think we should keep going. I promise to keep things professional."

That was unfortunately the last promise he wanted her to make.

"Fine," he said, knowing she was right about the time constraints.

"Good. You can do this, Nick. You're a little hard on yourself and too impatient. Some things take time to learn, to master. I'm sure you're used to instant success, but I've seen students far worse than you become excellent dancers."

"Far worse?" he challenged.

She tipped her head. "Okay, a little bit worse. But I believe in you."

Her sparkling brown eyes and the conviction in her voice warmed him in ways he couldn't even begin to admit. It had been a very long time since anyone had told him they believed in him. He'd chased that kind of approval for too long, and it had never come. He'd thought he didn't care anymore, but strangely he did.

"Nick?" she queried. "Did I say something wrong?"

"No," he said quietly. "You said it exactly right. You're a good motivator, Isabella."

"I wasn't trying to sell you, Nick."

"Either way, it looks like we're going to keep dancing. That's what you wanted."

"And what you want, too," she reminded him.

As they returned to the living room, he wondered why what he wanted wasn't as clear as it used to be.

Five

Isabella woke up Saturday morning to the ringing of her cell phone. Blinking her sleepy eyes open, she grabbed it off the end table and said, "Hello?"

"If you want to see the available rooms I have at the hotel, I can meet you there this morning," Nick said shortly.

She sat up in bed. "What are you talking about?"

"I'm at the Grand View Towers, my hotel on California—the one with a ballroom that might work for your dance classes."

"Of course. Sorry." She glanced over at the clock. "It's only seven-thirty."

"Did I wake you?"

"Yes, because it's Saturday, and it's only seven-thirty."

"I've been at work for over an hour."

"On Saturday?"

"I think we've established it is Saturday," he said dryly. "Look, the rooms are booked up later today for weddings and meetings. If you come down by eight, I can show you what will be available during the week. It's up to you. We can forget the whole thing. It would certainly be less work for me."

"No, I can come," she said quickly.

"Great. My office is on the fifteenth floor. Stop by the

concierge desk, and they'll give you a card key to get upstairs."

"Okay, thanks." She ended the call, took a deep breath, and then scrambled out of bed. She had a feeling that if she were a minute late, Nick would rescind his offer.

She jumped into the shower for a quick minute, then dried off, ran the blow drier through her hair and put on a dress and wedge sandals. She grabbed a cab to get across town, arriving at the Grand View Towers two minutes after eight. Not bad, she thought, as she headed into the magnificent hotel.

The hotel sat at the top of Nob Hill and had once been one of the great mansions of San Francisco. Massive renovations had turned it into a fifteen-story, five-star hotel with every luxurious amenity imaginable. Just walking into the spectacularly beautiful lobby took her breath away.

Exquisitely cut glass chandeliers hung from ornately carved and painted ceilings, and the slick marble floors were accented with richly woven carpets. She'd thought Nick's home had been impressive, but the hotel was beyond anything she had ever imagined.

Nick's company had taken over the hotel seven years earlier after it had begun to flounder in an economic crash. He'd obviously infused a lot of cash into the place to bring it up to its current standards, which made her wonder just how Nick had gotten started. She'd tried to ask him the day before, but he'd evaded her question. She should have done a little more research on him, or at least asked Ricardo for more details, but she wasn't one to stalk people on the Internet. She preferred to find out who a man was from the man himself, and she had to admit she was becoming very curious about Nick.

But that was a conversation for another day. She couldn't pry into his life when she was trying to get him to do her a huge favor. After seeing the magnificence of his hotel, she was surprised Nick would even consider letting her use a room for free. But he'd called her to come down, so she was going to take whatever help he wanted to offer her.

Stepping up to the concierge desk, she gave her name and was promptly awarded with a card key that would enable her to access the fifteenth floor.

The elevator walls were mirrored glass, and as she looked at herself, she couldn't help feeling like she was way out of her element. She'd grown up in dance studios and had spent most of her adult life working in the theater. The world of business was foreign to her, but if she was going to transition into a studio owner, she would have to learn how to be a businesswoman and not just a dancer.

As she stepped off the elevator, her spike heels sank into thick, plush carpet. She made her way over to a reception desk that was manned by a beautiful young woman with dark red hair and brown eyes. After taking her name, the woman gave her a friendly smile and waved her toward the door behind her desk.

Stepping into Nick's office was yet another adventure into the land of the rich and famous. His office, with its floor-to-ceiling windows, offered a sweeping view of San Francisco and the Golden Gate Bridge. But it was the man in the black leather chair who commanded her attention.

As he got up and walked around his massive desk to greet her, she couldn't stop the jolt of awareness that ran through her body. It was Saturday, but he still wore work clothes, charcoal gray slacks and a button-down shirt with a light plaid print. His only concession to the weekend was the lack of a tie.

He was so attractive with his dark hair and light blue eyes. His strong jaw spoke to his determined will, and his lips reminded her of the passion they'd shared the night before.

But that passion simmered beneath a very cool and controlled exterior. She didn't know Nick very well, but she sensed that he was a complicated man. She tried to tell herself that was why he wasn't *her* kind of man, but that would mean that rich, attractive, successful businessmen were not her type, and that sounded foolish even in her own head.

"Isabella," he said in his beautifully male baritone. "You made it."

"I know I'm a few minutes late, but you really didn't give me that much time."

"Short notice, I'm aware, but I didn't want you to miss this opportunity "

"I appreciate that." She paused. "This office is really nice."

"The perks of being the owner. Why don't you sit down for a moment?"

"I thought you were in a hurry."

"There's something I want to talk to you about first. You should sit."

His suggestion made her nervous, but she followed him over to a cozy seating area, sitting down on the sofa while he sat in the adjacent chair. He drew in a breath and let it out, a frown of uncertainty drawing his brows together.

"Well?" she asked.

"I have a proposition for you."

"That sounds ominous."

"It's not really."

"Then why is it taking you so long to speak?"

He acknowledged her point with a tip of his head. "Okay, here it is. As you know I have to dance the tango in Argentina a week from tomorrow. I'm going to need a partner, and I'd like that person to be you."

Her stomach turned over. "You want me to go to Argentina with you?" That was a crazy and terrible idea.

"Yes. I'll pay for your trip. First-class flight, luxury accommodations, extra days to travel if you want. And I'll also pay you well for your time."

She could barely take in the details. This invitation wasn't just about accompanying Nick on a business trip; it was about Argentina. He was going to her birthplace, to the country where her father still lived—the father she hadn't seen in over a decade. An emotional knot filled her throat. "I don't think so."

"Don't answer so quickly," Nick said. "Let's talk about it."

"I don't think there is anything to talk about."

"Oh, but there is. In exchange for your accompanying me to Argentina and being my dance partner, I'm prepared to offer you space in the ballroom for your dance classes for the next month at no charge." He paused. "I would also be happy to discuss investing in your studio. There might be a way we can work out a loan arrangement that will allow you to buy the studio from your aunt. That, however, would require some further research, so I can't guarantee an investment, but I would be willing to talk to you about it."

"You're pulling out all the stops." She felt overwhelmed by his offer.

"I know what I want, and I know how to get it," he said forcefully.

"If you were going anywhere else, I would have already said yes. But you're going to Argentina. I told you about my father, about his absence in my life. The memories I have of my home country are bittersweet and painful. I don't think I can go back there, not for any amount of money in the world or because of your enticing offer."

Even as she said the words, she wondered what the hell she was doing. The man was offering to solve all her problems for one short trip to Argentina and one even shorter dance.

"You don't have to see your father," Nick said. "It's a big country. He won't know you're there unless you want him to know."

"I wouldn't want to see him."

Nick stared back at her. "Are you sure about that?"

"Pretty sure. Of course I've thought about it, but I always came to the conclusion that it would be a mistake to reconnect with him. He deserted me. Maybe he had reasons to divorce my mother, but he should have tried to stay in my life."

"Staying in your life isn't the same thing as being a father."

There was a hard note in his voice now, and she saw something in his eyes that surprised her. He was very good at hiding his emotions, but there was a flicker of pain behind his words. "Are you close to your father?" she asked.

He shook his head. "No."

"But he's in your life?"

"If you're asking if he and my mother stayed together, the answer is yes. But if you're asking if I grew up in a happy family and had a great relationship with the man who fathered me, the answer is no. I've been Thomas Hunter's greatest disappointment."

"How is that possible? Look at you. Look at what you've accomplished."

"It's not what my father wanted. He wanted me to take over his business—he's a venture capitalist and runs a successful financial firm. I chose to go my own route. He wasn't happy about that."

"What about your mother? Are you close with her?"

"My mother died when I was eighteen."

"Oh, I'm sorry. I didn't know."

"Of course you didn't. Let's get back to you. I need you,

Isabella. And I'm willing to do whatever it takes to get you."

For a split second, she wished he needed her for more than a dance partner, but that was a foolish thought. This hard, driven man was not the kind of man she wanted in her life. He thought he could buy people. He hated emotion. He was all about money. They were as different as two people could be.

Yet, there was something they shared, a disappointment in their relationships with their fathers. It was a tenuous connection, but she related to the pain she'd heard in his voice earlier. Nick knew something about not being loved the way he'd wanted to be. And so did she.

"Isabella?" he pressed.

"I don't know."

"If you're worried that what happened last night might happen again, I can assure you that it won't. I will respect your boundaries."

She hadn't been worried about him trying to kiss her again, but now that he'd mentioned it, he'd just given her another reason to say no. The attraction between them would probably only grow with more time spent together. And that attraction couldn't lead anywhere.

"Let me think about it," she said finally.

It was clearly not the answer he wanted, but he reluctantly accepted it. "All right. I'll show you the ballroom. That might change your mind."

As they went down in the elevator together, she felt like she couldn't quite get her balance. While her body was in San Francisco, her mind was in Argentina.

Should she reconsider her quick refusal?

Her mother would not like to see her go to Argentina, and out of respect to her mom and all the hard work she'd put in over the years to give her a happy life, she should stick to her original decision.

On the other hand, she was an adult now, and if she wanted to reconnect with her father, she should be able to do that.

"Isabella, are you coming?" Nick asked, his hand holding the elevator doors open.

"Yes," she said, suddenly realizing that they'd arrived at the Mezzanine level.

The ballroom was just a few yards away from the elevator and as they stepped through the double doors, she was once again blown away by the size and the opulence of the room.

"It's huge," she murmured.

"We can close it off to a quarter of this size and install a hardwood floor. Mirrors and possibly a ballet barre could be rented."

"Yes, they could," she murmured, thinking that the space would be perfect, and the price was definitely right.

She turned to face him. "What if I don't go to Argentina with you? Does this all go away?"

He hesitated. "No. I'll still let you use the room for four weeks. But you won't get the cash for accompanying me on the trip, and I won't be able to invest in your studio."

He was still being extremely generous.

"I really want you to think about my offer," he continued. "You don't have to see your father. It's a big country. I seriously doubt you'll run into him."

"I'm not worried about running into him. I'm worried about *wanting* to run into him."

He met her gaze. "Maybe that would be good. You could get closure."

"I don't need closure. I need distance."

"You've had distance," he reminded her.

"And why would I want to change that?" she asked, feeling herself weakening. Over the years, she'd definitely thought about her homeland, and not just her father. She had some special memories of her time there. Did she dare to go back?

What was she so afraid of? She didn't have to see her father or any of her relatives. No one would know she was there. And it would be a short trip.

If she said yes, a lot of her problems would be solved. Was she really going to let her father steal anything else away from her? What would she be proving by staying away? That she was too scared to be in the same country as him? That was unacceptable.

"All right," she said. "I'll go."

Relief flooded his gaze. "You're sure?"

"Yes, but I want everything in writing, at least about the dance space and my salary for the trip."

"I'll have an agreement drawn up this weekend. You won't be sorry."

"I hope not, but I have to be honest, my stomach is churning right now. I feel a little sick."

"Maybe you're hungry. I haven't had breakfast. Have you?"

"No, because someone demanded I get down here in thirty minutes."

He offered an apologetic smile. "Let me buy you breakfast. I know a good place not too far from here."

"Not far from here?" she echoed. "I'm surprised you wouldn't take me to the hotel restaurant."

"It is excellent, but I have somewhere else in mind if you're game."

"Lead the way." If she was going to trust him to take her to Argentina, she could trust him with choosing a place to eat.

He held the ballroom door open for her and gave her a warm smile as she passed through. Since she'd agreed to go to Argentina with him, he'd visibly relaxed.

Maybe she'd have a chance to get to know the real Nick over breakfast. It might help her figure out how to get him to loosen up and embrace the tango. If he did let down his guard, he might be amazing.

There was a lot simmering beneath the surface of Nick Hunter. She just wondered if she was brave enough to go digging.

Six

Nick took Isabella down to the garage where his silver Mercedes convertible awaited. Once inside, he lowered the top and said, "It's a beautiful day. We might as well enjoy it."

"Sounds good to me," she said, as he drove out of the garage. "I must say I didn't really expect you to drive a convertible." She grabbed a band out of her bag and pulled her hair back into a ponytail.

He liked that he'd surprised her, because he knew her opinion of him wasn't that high. He couldn't blame her. He'd been a stiff-necked ass the last twenty-four hours, but now that she'd agreed to go to Argentina with him, he felt like he might actually be able to dance the tango and buy the land he wanted so badly.

"What kind of car do you drive?" he asked.

"I don't have a car at the moment. My apartment building charges a lot for parking spaces, so I take the bus or use a car service. It's a lot easier now that I don't have to stand out in the street and flag down a taxi. I can just go on my phone and call the nearest car."

"Technology eases our lives once again," he murmured.

"So where are we going?" she asked as he drove down a steep hill toward the bay.

"Sausalito. A friend of mine owns a café on the water. She makes incredible waffles."

"Friend as in girlfriend?" she asked curiously.

"Friend as in friend."

"It's hard to believe you're single and unattached. What's wrong with you?" she teased.

"I've been told I'm too dedicated to work, not sensitive enough, and very unforthcoming with personal details."

"Well, at least you have some self-awareness," she said dryly. "Do you agree with that assessment?"

"I have been all those things," he admitted. "Building my business has not left me a lot of time for personal relationships. I've been a bad date and a worse boyfriend. So it's not really that surprising I'm single."

"Don't you want more in your life than just a business? I doubt your hotels will keep you warm at night."

"Someday, but not today. Surely, you can understand that. All of your goals appear to be business related."

"That's a good point."

"So what about you?" He shot her a quick look. "Why are you still single?"

"Well, I'm not as old as you are, for one thing," she said with a laugh. "I'm only twenty-seven. I have plenty of time."

"I'm not that far ahead of you at thirty-three."

"You've really accomplished a lot for your age, Nick. I looked you up online last night, and your credentials are quite impressive."

"You looked me up?"

She gave an unrepentant shrug. "I like to know who my students are. I have to say, while I learned a great deal about your business, there wasn't much about you. I guess your former girlfriends kept their criticisms private. Aside from a few photos of you and super models, there wasn't much personal information."

"Like I said, I'm busy—so busy the tabloids can't keep up with me."

"I can't imagine what it would be like to have to dodge the press."

"It's not fun to have camera flashes going off in your face and any woman you happen to stand next to proclaimed as the new love of your life."

"Fame and money come with a cost."

"They do," he said, and he wasn't just talking about the press.

Isabella gave a little sigh as he drove over the Golden Gate Bridge.

"Look at the view." She waved her hand toward the bay. "You can see forever; nothing but blue sky and blue water."

"I'll take your word for it," he said, focusing on the Saturday traffic to Sausalito.

"I haven't been out of the city in a few months. Sometimes I forget that there's another world away from San Francisco."

"You'll be seeing more of the world very soon."

"When exactly are we leaving for Argentina?"

"Friday afternoon. It's a long flight, we'll get in Saturday morning. The performance is on Sunday night. We can fly back Monday, or if you'd like more time to explore, you can stay longer. Does that work?"

"Yes, I was worried that it might be at the same time as my friend's bridal shower, but that's the following weekend. I definitely cannot miss the shower, as I'm one of the bridesmaids. And Liz would probably kill me."

"You'll be back by then. Is Liz a long-time friend?"

"Since college. I made some of closest friends my freshmen year in the dorms. We've stayed close since then."

"That's impressive. Most people drift apart."

"We worried about that, so we made a pact. No matter where we are or what we're doing we'll always stand up for each other at our weddings. Three down and five to go."

"There are eight of you?"

"Yes, one bride and seven bridesmaids at every wedding."

"I've really never understood the concept of a huge bridal party. If a bride or groom needs that many people to get them down the aisle, maybe they shouldn't be getting married."

Isabella laughed. "That's not the point of it. It's about being surrounded by your friends and feeling their love and support."

"You should only need the love and support of the person you're exchanging vows with."

"Well, that's true. Liz doesn't need us, but she wants us to be there, and we want to be there for her."

"And everyone is showing up?"

She nodded. "So far, it's worked out, but I have to admit there's been a flurry of engagements lately so it's getting a little crazy. Laurel and Andrea got married last year. Liz is tying the knot in June, and Julie is planning a November wedding for when her fiancé gets done with baseball."

"Who is her fiancé?"

"Matt Kingsley."

"Really? Your friend is marrying the Cougar's star hitter?"

"Yes. He's a great guy. Do you like baseball? I might be able to get us tickets to a game."

"The hotel has season tickets, and I love baseball. I used to play when I was a kid."

"What position?"

"Pitcher."

"Of course. You would like to be in a position to control the game."

"I did like pitching," he admitted. "But the catcher actually calls the game, so the pitcher doesn't have all the power."

"Close enough."

"No sports for you?"

"Just dance. Anything that involved hitting or kicking a ball was not in my skillset."

He liked how honest and self-deprecating Isabella was. She never tried to portray herself in a more positive light. She was happy in her own skin, and he hadn't met too many people like that.

"Liz was one of the best athletes in our group," Isabella continued. "She's a little like you—ambitious, competitive, and always wants to be the best. Fortunately, she also has a big heart and a fiercely loyal streak where her friends are concerned."

"What does her fiancé do?"

"He's in public relations now. So is Liz. In fact, they work together at Michael's sister's company. But Michael used to be a pro football player, and I think his aspirations lie more in coaching than in promotions."

"What's his last name?"

"Stafford."

He nodded. "I've heard of him. What is it with your friends and professional athletes?"

She laughed. "I have no idea. But Liz and Michael met in high school, long before he was a famous football player. They actually didn't like each other when they were kids. I guess what they say about love being the flip side of hate is true. Once Liz and Michael reconnected and got past the old rivalries, there was nothing but love." She paused. "Liz is getting married at the Stratton Hotel in Sonoma. My friend Maggie works there and got her a deal. Do you know the hotel?"

"I do. I tried to buy it a few years ago, but the owner wouldn't sell. Apparently, she has a personal attachment to the place."

She glanced over at him. "You make that sound unusual. Don't you have a personal attachment to your hotels?"

"I love my hotels, but if it made sense to sell one, I would. If it's good business, I can't let emotion get in the way."

She sighed. "I don't think I'm going to be a good businesswoman. I often let emotion get in the way. Just the other day I agreed to let two girls take lessons for free because they gave me a sob story about their single mom. I later found out they had two wonderful parents who just didn't want to spend money on dance until they got their grades up."

"Did you kick them out?"

"No, because I thought if they wanted to dance that much, they should be dancing. I did, however, speak to their parents, and we worked out a schedule where the girls have to do their homework before they dance. That way we all win."

"And the parents agreed?"

"The mom said yes right away, but the dad kept saying dance was frivolous and the girls were wasting their time."

"Well, isn't it a little frivolous?" he couldn't help asking.

She frowned. "No. Dance is an art. Art is an important part of our culture."

"But it doesn't pay the bills."

"Sometimes it does."

"Not for most dancers." He wondered more about her background. "You said you danced professionally before you got injured. Was that lucrative?"

"I wasn't getting rich, but I could get by."

"And you've never thought about going back to the theater?"

"I'm a teacher now."

He didn't usually like to dig that deep into a woman's life, but her restraint was only making him more curious. "It feels like you're leaving something out of your story."

"I wasn't telling you a story," she returned. "I was a dancer. I'm not anymore. That's it."

"And you don't miss dancing?"

"I dance every day with my students."

"That's not the same thing."

"Dance is dance; it doesn't matter where you are or who you're doing it with." She paused, gazing over at him. "You'll see, Nick. Once you stop worrying about making the right steps, you'll fall in love with dance."

"I seriously doubt that," he said, pulling off the freeway at the Sausalito exit.

If he was going to fall in love, it wasn't going to be with dance, but it might just be with Isabella.

That errant thought sent a disturbing wave of uneasiness through his head.

He didn't do love. He didn't get attached.

And Isabella was the type of woman would settle for nothing less than a man's heart and soul—definitely not the woman for him.

—→➤◄←—

The Seagull Café was a tiny restaurant by the harbor in Sausalito. It looked more like a house than a restaurant with blue siding, white shutters and window boxes filled with flowers. Isabella was surprised by Nick's choice. The café looked warm and homey, not at all sophisticated, not at all the kind of place someone like Nick would go for breakfast.

But it was immediately clear that he was a regular at the café. A fifty-something-year-old woman with a round figure, sparkling blue eyes, and a cheerful smile greeted Nick with a big hug, an embrace he actually returned with some enthusiasm.

"It's been too long, Nicholas," she said. "Your table has missed you."

"I'm sure you've been able to fill it." He looked around the crowded café. "Business is good?"

"Very good, especially on the weekends." She gave Isabella an interested look, and said, "Aren't you going to introduce me, Nick?"

"Sorry. Isabella Martinez, this is Joanie Hooper. Joanie and her husband own this wonderful restaurant."

"It's nice to meet you," she said, seeing Joanie give her an assessing look.

"You, too," Joanie replied. "Your table is being bussed right now, Nick, so your timing is perfect."

"Any table will do," Nick said, but Joanie insisted on leading them to the outside deck and a table by the railing overlooking the boats.

"Whatever you want is on the house," Joanie added, handing them both menus. "The chef's special waffle of the day is blueberry, and it's amazing."

"You say that about everything Tom makes," Nick said.

"I found a good man, what can I say? My chef, Tom, is also my husband," she explained for Isabella's benefit. "We opened this café three years ago—with Nick's help. We couldn't have done it without him."

"You could have done it without me; it just would have taken you longer," Nick said.

"Like a lifetime." Her eyes welled up. "We owe you everything, Nick. I never would have imagined the serious, skinny kid who asked me a million questions would one day be my savior." She turned to Isabella. "He's a good man, in case you were wondering."

Isabella smiled. "Good to know."

"You don't have to impress her, Joanie," Nick said. "She's not a date. She's a…business associate."

"Really? Is that what I am?" she teased. She glanced up at Joanie. "Actually, I'm a dance teacher, and I'm teaching Nick the tango."

Joanie raised an eyebrow. "The tango? You're learning to dance, Nick? Now that sounds like a story I want to hear."

"I'll tell you another time," Nick said firmly. "We're kind of hungry here, Joanie."

"Okay, I'll let you off the hook for now. Why don't I bring you a couple of our favorite dishes, some omelets, waffles, bacon and hash browns. What do you say?"

"Sounds good to me," Isabella said, handing back her menu. "But what are you bringing for Nick to eat?"

Joanie laughed. "I like you, Isabella." She gave Nick a pointed look. "She's a lot more fun than those skinny models you usually show up with. They don't eat a thing. It's a waste of good food."

As Joanie moved away from the table, Isabella said, "Skinny models, huh?"

He shrugged. "I don't remember."

"Now that is a lie. You are not a man who forgets anything."

"You think you know me well enough to make that statement?"

"I don't know you well at all, but I still think I'm right."

He laughed. "Maybe this time."

His grin transformed his face from rigid and unyielding to friendly and warm.

"You should do that more often," she said. "Smile. It makes you look like a human."

"Otherwise, I look…"

"Angry, on your guard, as if you're ready for the worst."

He sat back in his seat, a contemplative gleam in his eyes. "I am usually ready for the worst. You read people well, Isabella."

"Sometimes. Not always. I'm trying to get better so I can save myself from painful mistakes."

"Who was he?" Nick asked.

The sharp gleam in his eyes told her he wasn't going to let her get away without an answer. "Carter Hayes."

"What happened?"

"A lot."

"Tell me."

She could have said no. Nick didn't like to talk about himself. He probably would have respected her privacy, but for some reason she found herself wanting to tell him. Maybe then he'd understand why the studio was so important to her.

"I met Carter in New York. He was getting a reputation for being a brilliant director, and I was awestruck when I met him. I was that foolish, naïve girl who couldn't believe the most popular man in the theater world wanted to date me. I thought I was special, but it turned out I wasn't. But I didn't find out right away. I was living in a dream world for several months."

"What do you mean?"

"We'd been going out a few months when a part came up in a new musical Carter was directing for a successful husband and wife production team—Hal and Donna Tyler. Carter got me an audition, and I won the role. It turned out to be a bigger part than either of us expected. Over the next few weeks, as the script got rewritten, my part got bigger. The Tylers and I were on the same page. I loved their musical and they loved the way I danced."

She took a sip of her water, then continued. "Carter, however, was not so happy. He didn't want me to have the bigger part. He was afraid to risk his reputation on an unknown, even an unknown he was sleeping with."

"Sounds like a hell of a guy."

"It took me far to long to see that he was not a good

person and he was never in love with me. I was just one of many women he liked. I actually found him in bed with another dancer—a friend. It was heart-breaking." She could still remember the pain and sense of betrayal she'd felt at that moment. "I thought that was the worst of it, but it wasn't."

"What else happened?"

"While my personal life was spinning out of control, my professional life also ran into problems. The production lost one of the stars three weeks before the opening to a serious illness. The investors got worried. One of them pulled his money out. The producers were scrambling to replace those funds. They wanted to put on a special showcase to generate excitement in the musical and sell more tickets for opening night. Carter had a lot of pressure on him, and he put that pressure onto me."

She swallowed a knot in her throat, then forced herself to continue. She'd gone this far, she might as finish the story. "There was a scene that involved a staircase and some scaffolding. In the rehearsal, I told Carter that I didn't think the structure was stable. He basically told me to suck it up and do the dance or he'd find someone to replace me. I saw the ruthless determination in his eyes. So I sucked it up, and I did the dance. Thirty seconds before the end of the number, the scaffolding collapsed, and I fell ten feet to the stage. I broke my leg in two places."

Nick drew in a quick breath. "Isabella, I'm sorry."

"I had to have surgery and months of rehab. Dancing was out of the question. So I went back to the studio and I started to teach."

"How long ago was that?"

"A year and a half."

"So you're fully recovered now?"

She nodded. "Yes, but I missed my window of opportunity. I'm old for a dancer now. I don't know that I could compete anymore, even if I wanted to, and I don't want to. I'm done with that part of my life. I'm going to run my own studio now, help other dancer reach their dreams." She let out a breath. "That's the whole story."

"What happened to Carter and the production after your injury?"

"It was shut down. Theater people can be very superstitious. No one wanted to touch the show. Carter went on to direct something else. The producers went on to produce something else. Time moved on."

"Why wasn't there a lawsuit?"

"The producers paid my medical bills. I had a lawyer for a while, but there was no indisputable evidence that the scaffolding had collapsed. There was an argument that I'd tripped and fallen, and with that fall, the structure had come down."

"It doesn't sound like you had a good lawyer."

"Probably not, but to be honest I just wanted to move on, too. The Tylers had been good to me. I didn't want to hurt them. I didn't want to put them out of business."

"And Carter? Did you forgive him?"

"I've really tried to forgive him for my fall. I don't believe that he honestly thought anything was wrong with the scaffolding when he sent me up there to dance. He should have listened to me, and he didn't, but he also didn't put the scaffolding together."

"But you told him it was unstable, and he shut you down."

"That's true. That's why forgiveness has been difficult. But I don't want to waste my life hating Carter for anything that he did, because that would just keep the pain fresh, and I need it to go away, not linger. I can't change what happened. I can only go forward. I'm fine now. I have a good life. The past is the past."

She was relieved to see a waiter with their food. She needed to put some pancakes into her churning stomach and turn the conversation in another direction.

"This looks amazing," she said. "I don't know where to start, waffles, pancakes, eggs?"

Nick smiled. "Start wherever you like. I'm sure we can get more if we run out of food."

"I don't think we'll run out. This is a feast." She popped a piece of bacon into her mouth. It was perfectly crisp. "I think this café was an excellent investment for you."

"Contrary to popular opinion," he said.

"What does that mean?"

"Nothing. Let's just eat."

She was happy to go along with that suggestion—at least for the moment. But when they'd finished off most of the plates, she decided it was only fair that Nick share a little personal information. "What did you mean before when you said investing in this café went against popular opinion?"

"My father thought it was a bad idea. Joanie had originally approached his firm. But when he said no, she came to me."

"Because you two knew each other?" she ventured, sensing that Joanie hadn't just been a stranger on the street.

"We did know each other. Joanie was my nanny when I was nine years old. She was with my family until I was fourteen. Then she took another job with some younger kids and eventually fell in love, got married, and decided to open a restaurant."

She was more than a little surprised to learn that Joanie had been Nick's nanny. It was hard to think of Nick as a child.

"She still tries to mother me," Nick said. "But I let her get away with it, because in reality she spent more time with me than either of my parents. My mom was a sweetheart, but when my dad said jump, she jumped. That usually meant she was with him and not with me. But Joanie was there." He sat back as the waiter cleared their table. "Do you want anything else?"

"No, I'm stuffed. It was all really good. I like that you helped out your former nanny, Nick. It's sweet."

He grimaced. "No one has ever described me as sweet."

She laughed at his disgruntled expression. "Well, in this instance, you were. Before you told me about Joanie, I didn't think you had any soft edges."

"I really don't, Isabella. Joanie was the exception."

She wondered if that were true. Before five minutes ago, she would have said yes, but now she wasn't so sure that Nick didn't have a side that very few people got to see.

Seven

After breakfast, they decided to take a walk instead of going straight back to the car. The path in front of the restaurant took them along the harbor, and as Nick looked out at the sailboats, he felt an odd, yearning desire to get on one of those boats and sail into the horizon with Isabella at his side.

It wasn't the kind of dream he had often or ever. In fact, he rarely dreamed at all anymore. Every day was about meeting whatever goal he had set the day before. He'd been running at a dead sprint for the past decade. He'd been happy in his ambition and mostly satisfied with his success, but today he felt restless.

He worked most nights and weekends. Self-made men didn't take days off. But today he didn't feel like going back to his office, and part of that reluctance had to do with Isabella. She was interesting and different, not at all like the women he usually spent time with, and he was intrigued. He also couldn't get their impulsive but passionate kiss the night before out of his head. And having her story about her bad love affair and her horrific injury, he felt an even stronger connection to her.

Isabella was a survivor, soft on the outside but very strong on the inside. He had a feeling she didn't even realize her strength, which made her even more appealing.

Isabella paused and rested her arms on a waist-high cement wall that edged the water. "I know I keep saying what a great view, but every time I turn around, my jaw drops," she said with a smile. "I spend most of days in a windowless studio with a mirror reflecting my movements. Sometimes I don't even know if it's sunny outside."

He could relate to that comment. Even though he sat in front of a huge window most of the day, he rarely looked out. He was too busy concentrating on whatever was on his computer or on a paper in front of him. And when he wasn't doing that, he was usually on the phone dealing with some crisis or closing a deal.

But today he was reminded that the city was more than his office building and had so much to offer from the magnificent skyscrapers of downtown to the trendy condos at the waterfront, the narrow, steep hills of Nob Hill and Russian Hill, to the broader streets of the Haight and the Sunset. In San Francisco, neighborhoods and cultures changed every block from Chinatown to Japantown to the predominantly Italian North Beach. The once mostly Irish Mission district now belonged to the twenty-somethings, and the hipster generation was settling in high-rise buildings south of Market. There was literally something for everyone in this town.

"I love this city," he murmured.

"Me, too," Isabella said, turning to look at him. "What else do you love?"

"What do you mean?"

"What excites you? What gets you up in the morning?"

"Making deals, increasing my net worth, growing my hotel chain." He knew she wouldn't like his answer. She wanted to hear something more soulful, but that's all he had.

"When will it be enough? What does success look like, Nick?"

He stared back at her, a little shaken by the question. "I don't know."

"You've never thought about it?"

"Not really. I still feel like I have a long way to go."

"To do what? Prove you're the best? Own the most hotels? Have the most money?"

"Those would all be good."

"But life isn't a game of Monopoly. What else do you want? What about marriage and children?"

"Possibly someday. I didn't grow up in the happiest of families, so I've never been in a rush to settle into some sort of long-term commitment. And not having had the greatest role model, I'm not sure I'd be a good husband or a father."

"You're not your dad."

"True."

"You said he was disappointed when you didn't go into his business, but it sounds like there's more behind your estrangement."

"I don't want to talk about him."

"Well, I didn't want to talk about Carter, but I did. I'm trying to get to know you and let you get to know me. I think it will help us when we dance together."

"That's a stretch."

"If you won't tell me about your father, then tell me about this land in Argentina that you want so badly. There are a lot of beautiful places in the world. What is it about that piece of property that makes you willing to undergo something so traumatic and painful as learning the tango?"

He smiled at her words. "You think I'm being overdramatic."

"Yes. So answer my question."

He debated for one long minute, then impulsively reached into his pocket and pulled out his wallet. From there he removed a folded piece of glossy paper. He opened it and handed it to her.

She gave him a look of surprise, then glanced down at the magazine picture of a beautiful sandy beach, a hammock slung between two palm trees, miles of clear blue sea, and one lone sailboat on the horizon."

"Is this the beach?" she asked.

"It is. It was named one of the best beaches in South America."

"The date on this page is from sixteen years ago." She looked up at him, a question in her eyes.

"Yes, it is," he said evenly, mentally preparing himself for what would come next.

She gazed into his eyes. "You've had this in your wallet for sixteen years?"

"Not quite that long." He hadn't really given conscious thought to how many years he'd been working towards his goal. "It hasn't always been in my wallet. I put it there when I went to Argentina a few weeks ago."

"What's the story behind this, Nick?"

He drew in a breath and slowly let it out. He'd never been tempted to show anyone that picture. Not even Martin knew what had driven him to that land in Argentina, but there was something about Isabella that made him want to open up.

"My mom cut that picture out of the magazine. She wanted to go there on vacation. She tried for a solid year to get my dad to take her there, but he was always too busy for a vacation. She told me once that she had the terrible feeling that if they didn't take that trip, their marriage would fall apart." His heart hardened at the memory. "But it wasn't their marriage that went bad; it was my mother's health. She got cancer. While that photograph had once started out as a way to save her marriage, it became the focal point of her battle to better health. She dreamed about going to that beach, resting on that hammock, sailing on that sea. She thought if she could just get there, everything would work out."

Isabella's eyes filled with moisture, and she put a hand on his arm in concern. "She didn't make it, did she?"

He shook his head, painful waves of emotion rolling through him.

"I'm so sorry, Nick. You don't have to talk about it if you don't want to."

Her words should have freed him from saying more, but while he hadn't wanted to talk about it at first, now he couldn't seem to stop the words flowing from his mouth. "After she died, we were packing up her things, and I took the picture off her bulletin board. I don't know why I kept it, but I couldn't bring myself to throw it away. We had so many talks about that beach. I felt like I had to get there for her—if for no other reason."

"It took you a long time to go."

"No, it didn't. I went the first time when I was twenty-two, right after I graduated from college. I fell in love with the beach. I vowed then and there that I'd find a way to own a piece of that land, but first I had to make some money. I wasn't interested in my father's offer to join his firm. I knew that he would try to make me over in his image, and I didn't think much of his image. I also didn't want to move money around for a living. That sounded very boring. I got a job in a hotel and started working my way up. I found that I loved the hotel business. Along the way, I made some valuable contacts with people who had money to invest in me and my dreams."

"Did your father help you at all?"

"No, he was angry that I didn't fall in line with his plans. He told me over and over again that I'd never make it."

"You proved him wrong."

"Yes, I did," he agreed. "Not that he'd ever admit it. In fact, he still gives my grandfather more credit than me."

"Why is that?"

"While my father wasn't interested in investing in my business, my mother's father did leave me a sizable nest egg when he died. That was the seed money for buying my first hotel. It was a boutique hotel in Southern California. It became extremely profitable. After that I acquired some partners and some venture capital. From there, I just kept going."

"You make it sound pretty easy, but there must have been hurdles. You're very young to have built so much."

He shrugged. "Apparently, I inspire confidence—when I'm not dancing, that is."

"Good point," she said with a smile. "Well, you should be extremely proud of yourself, of all that you've accomplished."

"I'm not where I want to be yet."

"Which brings us back to my original point. I wonder if you'll ever feel that you're where you want to be."

"I guess I'll find out. I've had my head down, pedal to the metal for a very long time. I can't remember the last time I took a day off and thought about anything but work."

"That's not good. Every life needs balance."

"Balance is overrated. It's just one more thing to work into the schedule."

She tipped her head in acknowledgement of his point. "So maybe not balance, but you still have to find a way to appreciate the moment you're in and not always be looking toward the next one and the one after that. Otherwise, you'll miss the life you're living."

"You like to live in the moment, don't you, Isabella?"

"I do," she admitted. "There are so many nuances to every minute, every conversation, every person you see or pass by. I don't like to rush my way through life. I like to savor things."

He'd like to savor her. That was one part of his life where

he liked to go slow.

"Unfortunately, my live-in-the-moment strategy sometimes leaves me open to unexpected problems," she continued.

"Like old pipes that suddenly break?"

She made a face at him. "I'm not taking sole responsibility for that. My aunt knows more about the plumbing than I do."

"Which might be why she wants to sell."

"I know the business has been weighing her down and her heart is not in it anymore. That's why I need to take it over. And apparently you're going to help me do that, or are you already reconsidering your proposition?"

He shook his head, thinking that investing in a small dance studio would barely be a blip on his financials. "Not at all. I told you I would consider investing in exchange for your agreement to go to Argentina."

"Which does seem fairly incredible, since all I have to do is dance the tango for about five minutes."

"But that tango gets me an incredible piece of property and will launch a five-star resort that will be unlike any other. It's all about money and value, Isabella. Life is about trade and negotiation."

She frowned at his words. "I think life is about more than that, and I believe you do, too. You like to put yourself forward as a cold, unemotional, somewhat ruthless, obsessively determined businessman, but this photo shoots all that to hell. Because no one who is all the things I just said would keep a photo from a magazine that his mom cut out sixteen years ago."

She had a point. He took the paper out of her hand and refolded it. Then he put it back into his wallet.

"Just because you put it away doesn't mean it's not there anymore," she teased.

"I'm aware that the photo is a weakness. I guess we all have one."

"Sometimes more than one. I have many."

"You're very honest, Isabella."

"I try to be. It's not as exhausting being honest as attempting to be someone I'm not."

He couldn't help thinking she was getting a little dig in, and maybe she was right. He did like to portray himself a certain way, and sometimes it was tiring, but it was worth it. He'd created a persona that investors wanted to invest in. He couldn't do what he did if he came across as sentimental or weak.

"I should get back to the hotel," he said.

"That's it? That's the end of our conversation?"

"I have work to do."

"And you don't want to admit that you have a softer side, do you?"

"Softer sides don't work well in business."

"They do in the tango."

"I didn't see much softness when you and Ricardo danced."

"Then you weren't looking close enough. Of course, there's the sharpness, the passion, the intensity, but as I told you before, it's a push-pull, it's a dance of contrasts, man and woman, hard and soft, passionate and tender."

He found his body tightening at her words. Whenever Isabella talked about dancing the tango, he started imagining those same moves taking place in the bedroom.

Clearing his throat, he said. "Let's walk back to the car."

"Okay," she said, giving the harbor one last wistful look. "It's such a nice day. I hate to leave."

He could relate, but he had work to do and he'd already told Isabella way too much about his past and his family. He needed to put some distance between them before he started forgetting exactly why he was with her.

—➤➤◄◄—

As they drove back to San Francisco, Isabella thought about what Nick had told her. He'd surprised her by showing her the magazine photo, by talking about his mother and her dreams, his father and his coldness. She was starting to understand Nick a little better now. And she was quickly beginning to see that the man had a lot of layers.

She wanted to unravel those layers, get to the core and see everything that he tried so hard to hide. He'd told her quite a bit, but she thought there was more. His father was still a mystery to her.

Not being happy that his son hadn't followed in his footsteps didn't seem like a strong reason for the animosity and distance between Nick and his dad. Nick obviously resented his father for not taking his mother to her dream beach and for not being present in his life, but she still felt like there was a missing piece of the puzzle.

She wasn't going to get any more out of him now, though. He'd shut down almost as quickly as he'd opened up. She couldn't really blame him. She didn't always want to talk about her family, either. Unfortunately, the upcoming trip to Argentina was going to make it impossible not to think about her dad, the missing parent in her life, the country she'd left behind as a small child.

Could she really go back there? Could she hear the familiar accents, see her own features replicated in so many others and not wonder how different her life would have been if her parents had not split up, if her mother had not brought her here to San Francisco?

She'd had a good life, though. She couldn't complain. Her mother had worked a lot, but her aunt had picked up the slack, and even though she wasn't extremely close to her mom, they talked on a regular basis. They got together for dinner at least once or twice a month.

They probably would have been closer if her mom had been willing to open up more about her dad. But her mother's silence on her father had always put a wall between them. She could accept that as a small child her mother had wanted to protect her from anything negative. But she'd grown up a long time ago, and she still couldn't get past the unspoken secrets of the past.

Her mother would not want her to go to Argentina and would probably be able to come up with dozens of reasons for why it wasn't a good idea, but Isabella didn't want to let her mother make this decision for her.

She would go back to where she'd been born. As to whether or not she would try to find her father was a question she couldn't yet answer.

"Why don't I take you home?" Nick suggested as they crossed over the bridge into San Francisco.

"Actually, if you could drop me off at the studio, that would save me a bus ride. I know it's not anywhere near the hotel—"

"Don't worry about it."

"Thanks."

"When is our next lesson?"

She thought for a moment. They needed as much time as possible to get Nick up to speed, but she had plans for the evening. "How about tomorrow night?"

"That should work."

"Good." As she thought about their next lesson, she knew she had to try something new and different to get Nick to relax and enjoy the dance. They'd gotten to know each other a little better the past few hours, but she had a feeling the walls would come back up as soon as she turned on the music tomorrow night.

An impulsive idea ran through her head. He'd say no. It wouldn't be his scene, his friends, his kind of night...

On the other hand, maybe he needed a different kind of night. He'd admitted that he'd been all work and no play for a long time, and that he rarely lifted his head to look around. Being that closed off was not going to help him master a dance of passion and exhibition.

"Nick," she said.

He gave her a wary look. "What?"

"Do you like to bowl?"

"Bowl?" he echoed as if she'd just asked him a question in a foreign language.

"As in throw a ball towards some pins and knock them over."

"I know what bowling is; I just haven't thought about it since I was twelve years old."

"There's a very cool bowling alley by the ballpark— Barker's Bowl. It's part of a bar/restaurant venue. Live music, strobe lights, slick lanes, designer shoes. It's not your father's bowling alley," she said with a smile.

"Are you asking me on a date, Isabella?"

"I'm inviting you to be part of a group that's going to the bowling alley tonight at nine to celebrate my friend Kate's birthday," she said quickly.

"Is she one of the brides-to-be?"

"No, she's one of the bridesmaids. There are about ten people going. We've reserved three lanes. It should be fun." She licked her lips when he didn't answer right away. "I'm sure it's not what you normally do on a Saturday night. It's more blue collar than white collar."

"Do you think I'm a snob?"

"I don't know."

"Most people would automatically say, of course you're

not a snob."

"I'm not most people."

"I'm beginning to realize that."

"Look, it's not a big deal. Forget I asked. You probably have a date anyway."

"Actually, I'd like to go. I do have a dinner with a business associate, but it should wrap up by nine or a little later."

"You can meet us at the bowling alley. If you decide you don't want to come, it's completely fine."

"I'll be there."

"Great," she said, hoping she hadn't made a mistake. Her girlfriends would be all over Nick with speculative questions, but maybe that was a good thing. It had been a while since she'd brought a hot date with her, and Nicholas was certainly one of the most attractive men she'd ever met, smarter than most, too, but his obsession with work and money made her wary. She respected ambition and drive in a man, but Nick was a little one-dimensional for her taste. Perhaps tonight she'd get to see another side of him.

Eight

Barker's Bowl was located in a huge building near the Cougars' ballpark and the southern seaport of San Francisco. In front was a restaurant with an enormous bar. In the back was a bowling alley made up of twelve lanes surrounded by comfortable couches and chairs. The alley lighting was a mix of purple and pink, and music blared across the speakers, adding a club-like feel to the room.

The bowling alley was crowded as it was most Saturday nights, and she and her group of friends had been sharing three of those lanes for the past hour. Changing partners and teams with each game, they'd also gone through a couple of rounds of drinks and a few bowls of pretzels, peanuts and chips.

Checking her watch, Isabella frowned when she realized it was after ten. Nick was an hour late, which probably meant he wasn't coming. He'd mentioned a dinner, and it was certainly possible that it had gone longer than he'd imagined. Or it was more likely that he'd had second thoughts about spending time with her and her friends.

Why would he want to bowl with a bunch of strangers and a woman who was just his dance teacher, a woman he'd met two days earlier? They weren't in a relationship. They weren't really even friends. She was just a means to an end for Nick, and she really shouldn't let herself forget that.

Kate Marlow, a slender brunette with sparkling blue eyes, came over, two glasses of white wine in her hand. She handed one of those to Isabella. "You look thirsty."

"Thanks. Are you having fun?"

"I am. One of the best birthday parties I've ever had. And it's nice not to be the organizer for a change."

"I'll bet." Kate was a wedding planner, and because she was so good at organizing events, she often planned their birthday parties as well.

"You, however, do not look like you're having as much fun as I am," Kate said, giving her a thoughtful look. "Is something wrong?"

"No, I'm just a little tired. It's been a long week."

"Julie told me that your studio got flooded. It sounds like a disaster."

"It's pretty bad. My aunt and I met with a couple of contractors this afternoon. They should have their bids in by Monday, but judging by the few comments they made, the repairs will be extensive. The flooding is actually the least of the problems. The plumbing and even some of the electrical wiring have to be redone."

"What does your aunt think?"

"That it's a really good time to get rid of the studio if the interested buyer she has doesn't go running in horror at these recent developments."

"Is that likely?"

"I'm not sure. She hasn't told me anything about the buyer." Isabella paused. "I have to admit I haven't asked her too much about the person, either. I really want her to sell to me."

"Still?" Kate quizzed. "Maybe you'd be better off finding another space and starting from scratch."

That was probably a logical suggestion, but her heart was in her aunt's studio. "We'll see. I need to take it one step at a time." Her gaze drifted across the room as she caught a glimpse of a man with dark hair making his way towards them, but it wasn't Nick.

"Maybe you should text him," Kate suggested.

"Who?"

"The man you're waiting for. Come on, Isabella. You've been checking your watch every fifteen minutes, and you mentioned something earlier about wanting to wait for your partner, so I can only assume you invited someone to come, and he hasn't shown up."

"I asked Nick Hunter. He's taking dance lessons from me."

Kate raised an eyebrow. "Nick Hunter—as in Nick Hunter who owns the Grand View Tower Hotel?"

"That's the one. I'm surprised Liz and Julie didn't already tell you that I'm giving him tango lessons."

"I'm surprised, too. I should have been the first one they called. So you invited him here—to bowling night?"

"I'm trying to get to know him better, so I can get him to relax when we dance."

"So dating your student to improve his dancing—interesting strategy," Kate teased. "What's really going on? Do you have a mad crush on him?"

"I'll admit that he's very attractive, and I like him. But since he's standing me up, I wouldn't get too excited about any romantic possibilities."

"Text him. See where he is. He could be lost."

"No, he knows where I am. He had a dinner tonight, so he was iffy about coming. It's not a big deal. And it's not really a date."

"Your eyes say that it's a big deal. You look disappointed, Isabella."

"Maybe a little, but it was an impulsive invitation. I didn't really expect him to say yes."

"What's he like?"

She thought about the simple question, wishing there was a simple answer. "Honestly, I'm still trying to figure him out. He has a very stiff, hard, unyielding side to his personality. But I've also seen glimpses of dry humor and the occasional warm smile. Sometimes I think he's having an ongoing battle with himself on what kind of man he wants to be."

"Well, you've thought a bit about him," Kate remarked with a knowing gleam in her eyes. "He's gotten under your skin."

"He intrigues me. I've never met anyone like him. But before you start planning our wedding, I have to tell you that he's a committed bachelor. He's been very up front about the fact that he lives for his job and his focus is on growing his hotel empire."

"Then why on earth did you invite him here? He's clearly a wealthy guy with a lot of options and no interest in relationships. That sounds like a player."

"It was a moment of temporary insanity. I actually don't know if he's a player. I think he's a little too serious for that. He doesn't live his life in a carefree way. Maybe I'm being naïve, but I don't see him having a lot of random hookups. He's very cautious about who he trusts, who he lets into his life. Anyway, enough about him, it looks like you and I will be partners for the rest of the night."

"I don't think so."

"Why not? Did I throw too many gutter balls earlier?"

Kate laughed. "You did, but I think your guy just showed up. And I must admit he's dream-worthy."

Isabella turned her head to see Nick making his way through the bowling alley. Her stomach clenched with a nervous tingle and her heart started beating a little faster. He had on slim-fitting gray slacks that hugged his lean legs and a light blue shirt that brought out the color of his eyes. Even though this wasn't his usual turf, he walked with confidence and purpose, and she could see more than one woman pause to look at him. But Nick didn't notice. His gaze was on her.

As their eyes met, a smile curved his lips, and her palms began to sweat—so much for pretending this wasn't a date or that she wasn't interested in him in a purely feminine way and didn't want another taste of his sexy mouth.

She drew in a breath and told herself to get it together. He was just a man. And she was used to being close with men. She was a dancer. She was extremely comfortable with her body and being in close contact with other people. But Nick wasn't other people...

"Hi," he said in a husky voice. "Sorry I'm late."

"It's fine." She could hear conversation and laughter all around her, balls running down the alleys, pins clicking as they tumbled to the floor and the steady beat of music wafting through the air, but everything was hushed in her mind, as if the rest of the world was very far away.

She couldn't seem to stop staring at Nick, and he couldn't seem to stop staring back.

Then she felt someone nudge her back.

"Aren't you going to introduce me?" Kate asked.

She started, suddenly realizing that Kate was watching them with extreme interest. "Sorry. Nick Hunter, this is Kate Marlowe, one of my really good friends."

"Nice to meet you," Kate said, shaking his hand.

"You, too. It's your birthday, isn't it?"

"It is," Kate said in surprise.

"I'm sorry I don't have a present, but I'd love to invite you and some friends to have dinner in the restaurant at my hotel one night. I don't know if you've been Prescott's before, but I think you'd enjoy it."

"I'd love that," Kate said. "The restaurant has an amazing reputation."

"Isabella knows how to reach me. Just let me know a good day and for how many, and I'll make sure you get first-class service."

"Very generous of you." Kate paused. "I think the next game will be starting soon. You two should play."

"I'll show you where to get some shoes," Isabella said. "If you're planning to bowl, that is."

"That's why I'm here," he said.

"You look a little happier about bowling than you did about dancing," she told him as she led him over to the counter to pick up some shoes.

"I haven't done it in a while, but I remember being good enough not to embarrass myself."

"Lucky you. I think I'm the worst one out here."

"These shoes are definitely not what I remember wearing as a kid," Nick said a few minutes later as they sat down on a bench behind the lanes, and he laced up his bowling shoes.

The shoes were a mix of orange, red and lime green and definitely took Nick's sophisticated appearance down about twelve notches, but she liked his new look.

"They suit you," she said.

He gave her a doubtful look. "I know you like to put a positive spin on things, but that's a stretch, even for you, Isabella."

She smiled. "I'm really glad you came, Nick."

"Me, too."

The look that passed between them sent a shiver down her spine.

"Hey, Isabella, you're up." Liz's voice broke the tension between them.

Isabella was beginning to think she should have invited Nick to a private bowling date.

"I'm Liz Palmer, and you're Nick Hunter."

"I am. Have we met?"

"Not really, but I used to work for Damien, Falks and Palmer. We did some promotional work for the Grand View Towers a few years back."

"Of course. Is your father Ron Palmer?"

"He is."

"I remember him. How's he doing? I think I heard he was ill?" Nick ventured.

"He's better now, thanks. My family also stayed in your hotel in Hawaii last year. It was beautiful."

"That is one of my favorite properties," Nick said. "It's a little smaller than most of my hotels but the location is excellent."

"It was perfect. I can't wait to go back," Liz said.

"Let me know when you can make it over there again; I'll make sure you get a deal."

"Great. You two are up for the next game."

"You don't have to offer all my friends perks," Isabella said as they stood up. "Dinner for Kate—a hotel in Hawaii for Liz. What's next?"

"Maybe something for you?"

"You're already doing something for me."

"That's business. Perhaps something more personal."

She was surprised and a little unnerved by his statement. "We should get you a bowling ball," she said, changing the subject, because she really didn't know what to say to his comment.

"I can throw whatever is there. They're all the same to me."

"Okay, good. It looks like we're going up against my friend Julie and her fiancé, Matt Kingsley. He had a home game this afternoon so he actually gets to hang out with us on a Friday night, which is rare."

She took Nick over to meet the rest of her friends. He fit in quite well and was much warmer and friendlier than she'd thought he would be. She didn't know if he was putting on a face or if this was the real Nick, but she liked this version of him more than the one who showed up for tango lessons.

But as they started to bowl, the more serious, competitive side of Nick resurfaced. He took every throw quite seriously, frowning when he didn't get a strike or pick up a spare. She was just happy when her ball stayed out of the gutter.

While she had drive and determination when it came to dance, she didn't really care that much about other sporting activities. She preferred to just enjoy herself rather than get caught up in winning, but it was clear that Nick liked to win.

So did Matt Kingsley, Michael Stafford and Alex Donovan. Soon, the four men were caught up in their own game, each striving to come out on top while the women drank wine and cheered them on.

"Do you think they even know we're still here?" Andrea joked.

A dark-eyed brunette, Andrea had married Alex several months earlier, and while she was usually the most competitive of the females present, she'd mellowed since she'd gotten married.

"I doubt it," Liz said dryly. "Boys and their games."

"It's nice they're all getting along," Julie said. She gave Isabella a pointed look. "Nick fits in well."

"I know. I wasn't sure he would."

"Another reason to like him," Kate said, elbowing her in the side.

"You're into him, just admit it," Liz put in.

"Liz is right," Julie said. "You haven't stared at a guy this much in years."

"And he's definitely worth a stare," Andrea agreed. "You have good taste."

"Stop," she said. "He just came to bowl."

"And to spend time with you," Kate reminded her.

At Kate's words, Isabella couldn't help wondering why Nick had come. Was it just to be nice to her, keep her happy until he got her to Argentina? Or had there been another reason? Well, it didn't really matter. She was going to stop analyzing and just enjoy the moment.

"One lousy pin," Nick said, coming over to her as their heated game ended. "I would have beaten Matt if that one damn pin hadn't stayed upright."

"There's always next time."

"I thought you were going to take me down, Nick," Matt said with a happy grin.

"You were too good for me."

"Please, don't make his head any bigger than it already is." Julie put an arm around Matt's waist. "You've had quite the day, Matt: a triple, a homerun, and now a bowling match. Do they call it a match?"

"I know they call it a win," Matt said with a laugh, giving Julie a quick kiss. "You're my lucky charm, babe."

"Well, your lucky charm needs something more substantial to eat than pretzels and popcorn. Anyone else up for some appetizers in the restaurant?"

A chorus of agreement followed Julie's words. After changing out of their bowling shoes they walked out to the restaurant. Isabella found herself squeezing into a big booth next to Nick. They talked and laughed, ate potato skins and chicken wings and drank their way through another carafe of wine.

A little before one, they made their way outside. After saying goodbye to her friends, she gave Nick a smile. "I'll get a cab home."

"I'll drive you. My car is just around the corner."

"Really? You found a parking spot nearby?"

"I got lucky."

"You seem to get lucky a lot," she commented as they walked down the street together.

"Actually, a buddy of mine owns the building with the parking structure and he gave me a pass to use when I go to the ballpark."

"Ah, so not exactly lucky."

He shrugged. "I guess not. Tonight was fun. Your friends are great. Not a pretentious one in the bunch. That was a nice change for me."

"Sounds like you need to mix up your social circle."

"I think that's what I was doing tonight," he said as they walked into the parking garage.

"I was a little surprised you agreed to come. Why did you?"

He paused by his car. "I seem to have trouble saying no to you."

"Really? I can't imagine why. A lot of people tell me no. As a dancer, I can't tell you how many times I've been rejected."

"Anyone who rejected you as a dancer had to be crazy."

"No, they just wanted something I didn't have. Casting directors can be brutal. They come back at you with harsh truths. Too short. Too tall. Too average. Bad feet. No style. Lacks expression. I've heard it all."

"You must have had to develop a thick skin."

"It did get pretty thick, but I'm human. No matter how much you tell yourself that it's just one person's opinion, sometimes the words sting." She waited for him to unlock her door, but he didn't seem in a hurry.

"Isabella," he began.

She gave him a wary look. "What?"

"You're beautiful and talented. Whoever said you weren't was wrong."

His words brought an emotional knot to her throat.

"Thanks," she murmured.

He ran his finger down the side of her cheek surprising her with the tender gesture. "You asked me why I came tonight, and the truth is—I couldn't stop thinking about you. About what happened between us last night."

"That was an impulsive moment."

"I want to be impulsive again."

"It's not an impulse if you talk about it first," she said lightly.

He smiled. "Good point. Why don't I do this instead?" He lowered his head and covered her mouth with his. This was no gentle caress but a demanding, possessive kiss from a man who was used to getting everything he wanted. And he obviously wanted her.

She'd never been one to hold anything back, but Nick stirred her emotions as well as her body, and that scared her. She wanted him, but she didn't want to have her heart broken, and she thought he might just have the power to do that.

So she'd pull away—in a second.

It was actually Nick who lifted his head first. He gazed down at her, his light blue eyes glittering in the shadowy parking garage.

She thought she should say something, but she didn't know what.

He seemed to have the same trouble coming up with words.

Finally, he said. "I should take you home."

She should have been relieved by his decision, but she felt restless and uncertain and a little annoyed that he seemed to think he was in charge. Then again, why wouldn't he feel in charge? He was always in charge.

"I'll get a cab," she said, pulling out her phone.

"Don't be ridiculous. I'll drive you." He opened the car door. "Get in."

"Don't order me around," she snapped.

He sighed. "Isabella, what's going on?"

Frustration and sexual tension were the two answers that came to mind, but instead she said, ""You don't get to decide what happens between us. It's not just *your* decision."

He stared at her. "What do you want to happen?"

She really should have just gotten in the car and kept her mouth shut. After a tense moment, she said, "I want to go home."

"I guess we're on the same page after all."

After giving him her address, they didn't speak on the drive across town. She didn't know how they had gone from laughing and having fun together to being completely awkward. Actually she did know—it was that incredibly damned good kiss and both of their reactions to it. She was as much to blame as he was, because she wanted him but didn't want to act on that need, and maybe he felt the same way.

He pulled up in front of her building and turned off the car. "Isabella, I think we should clear the air, and I should apologize."

She sighed. "There's nothing for you to apologize for."

"Are you sure about that? You seem angry."

"I'm being stupid."

"I don't think you're stupid," he said quietly. "I asked you before what you wanted. You didn't really answer me."

She met his gaze and couldn't give him anything but an honest answer. "I don't know, because you scare me a little, Nick."

"I would never hurt you, Isabella."

"You might not mean to, but I think you could."

"Or you could hurt me. Did you ever consider that?"

She hadn't, but even thinking about it now, she didn't believe that was possible. "I don't believe you'll let me get close enough to hurt you. But I would let you get close. I'd live in the moment, and open my heart, and when it ended I'd be unhappy."

"I thought you were the kind of woman who didn't worry about the future."

"I've been hurt before. I guess that tamed my free spirit. I'm more cautious now."

He nodded. "Why don't we just concentrate on being good dance partners for the next week?"

His practical words sounded good. "All right." She paused, her hand on the door. "Do you want to meet tomorrow?"

"I can do tomorrow evening if that works for you—around eight?"

"That will work. If we could do it at your hotel, we could try out the floor for Monday's classes."

"I'll see you there."

She hesitated, knowing she should just get out of the car and go into her apartment, but she still felt a little unsettled by all the emotions of the last thirty minutes. "Nick—I just want to say one thing."

"What's that?"

"That was a really good kiss."

He smiled. "I thought so, too. Goodnight, Isabella. Sweet dreams."

She had a feeling her dreams would be more sexy than sweet, and a certain dark-haired, blue-eyed man was going to be the star.

Nine

—➤➤◄◄◄—

While her dreams were delicious, Sunday brought Isabella back to reality. She spent the morning at the studio talking to contractors, reading estimates, and reworking the class schedule for the next week.

She had no idea where her aunt was. Rhea had left a message on her phone around ten that she'd stop by in the late afternoon, but so far Isabella had not seen her. That worried her. Rhea had never been a secretive person, and the fact that she was being a cagey about where she was and what she was doing made Isabella uneasy.

Was Rhea going to sell the studio as is? Was all her hard work going to be for nothing if a new buyer stepped in with his or her own plans?

She really needed to speak to her aunt. Nick had offered to help her buy the studio, and while that seemed like an enormous favor to her, maybe for him it was not even close to a big deal. When she saw him later, she'd have to ask him exactly what he had in mind.

She didn't really want to tie herself that closely to him or put herself in a position to owe him more than she could pay, but she really did want to save the studio. She was starting to feel a little desperate about it. If the studio went away, where would she go?

She didn't have another plan. Ever since she'd been

injured and her theater career had ended, the studio had been her safe haven. It was the next chapter in her career. While she could probably work for someone else and/or maybe eventually open a studio somewhere else, she couldn't imagine losing this particular dance space. It would be like losing a limb. She had so many memories in this place from the time she was a little girl until now.

Saying goodbye seemed unthinkable.

She looked up from the computer as Ricardo walked through the front door. He wore dark jeans and a gray knit shirt, his black hair damp from a probably recent shower. He looked tired, but there was also an odd light in his eyes.

"I didn't think you were coming here today," she said.

"I wanted to talk to you."

"I hope it's about how to get this studio fixed in record time?"

"Unfortunately, no. But I have some interesting news. I just got off the phone with Hal Tyler."

Her stomach tightened at the mention of her former producer. "Why would you be talking to Hal?"

"Hal and Donna are opening a new show in San Francisco at the end of August. It's a musical. James Bennett is directing. Malcolm Hodges is the choreographer."

A wave of nausea ran through her. She had a feeling she knew what Ricardo was about to say.

"They want us both to audition," he continued. "Donna said she was planning to call you. She was just waiting for their funding to finalize, and now it has."

Isabella immediately started shaking her head. "No, I'm a teacher now. I have classes to worry about. All these problems at the studio have to be dealt with. I can't audition. I don't want to audition. That isn't my life anymore."

Ricardo's lips drew into a tight line. "Isabella. Your aunt is going to sell the studio. You know that."

"Maybe I'll buy it."

"With what?"

"With Nicholas Hunter's money. He told me he might be interested in investing."

"Seriously? Why would he do that?"

"It would be an investment for him?"

"The king of hotels wants to invest in a dance studio? Just how close have you two gotten?"

"It's not like that. I'm helping him secure a business deal. In return, he wants to help me."

"Okay. Let's put that aside for the moment. This is your chance to get back on the stage, Isabella. The Tylers love you. They feel terrible that you were injured on their production."

"My accident shut down their show."

"Their poor set construction shut down the show. And that was also Carter's fault. He was taking shortcuts that they didn't know about." Ricardo paused, giving her a serious look. "There aren't many second chances in life, Isabella. You need to take this one."

"I'm not as good as I was. I haven't been dancing."

"You dance alone at night. I see you in the studio after classes."

"That's just for me."

"Just think about it. Don't say no. This is too big of an opportunity to dismiss out of hand. You have to give it thought."

She didn't want to think about going back to that life, because there was a part of her that wanted nothing more than to be the star she'd once dreamed about being. But there was another part of her that wanted to stay where it was safe, where she wouldn't fall—literally or metaphorically.

"What are you two talking about?" Rhea asked, interrupting their conversation.

Isabella was startled to see her aunt. "I didn't hear you

come in."

"You two were engrossed in conversation. What's going on?" Her curious gaze moved from Isabella to Ricardo. "Anyone want to share?"

"The Tylers are opening a new musical in San Francisco in a couple of months," Ricardo replied. "They want Isabella to audition, and I think she should."

Isabella sent Ricardo a killer look, but he didn't bat an eye. He obviously wanted Rhea on his side, and there was no doubt that her aunt would be there.

"That's amazing, Isabella," Rhea said. "Their musicals are always fantastic."

"I'm done with that part of my life. I want to teach. I want to run a studio. I don't need to perform any more. And I'm not good enough. I couldn't be what I was."

Rhea frowned. "You've completely healed from that injury, Isabella. Maybe you would need to put in some long hours, but you could get yourself back in shape. This actually comes at a good time. The repairs will be very expensive, Isabella. I've talked to my buyer, and she's willing to buy the studio as is for a lower price. I'm meeting with my accountant tomorrow to run the numbers. I don't think I can keep throwing good money after bad. This place has been a wonderful home for all of us, but sometimes you have to move on."

"I think I can buy the studio, too," she said. "I have someone willing to invest. Can you at least give me a few days to see if I can pull that together?"

"Who would want to invest in this place?"

"Nicholas Hunter. The man I'm giving tango lessons to."

"Seriously? Why?"

"Does it matter?" she countered, seeing the same confused look on her aunt's face as she'd seen on Ricardo's.

"I think it does. The man has already agreed to give you a

ballroom to run our classes in for the next few weeks. Now he wants to buy the studio? What are you giving him in exchange for all this good will? I know it's more than dance lessons."

She saw the worried gleam in her aunt's eyes. "It's not *that*," she said sharply.

"Then what?"

"Nick needs me to go to Argentina with him and dance the tango for some business investor. It's part of a deal he's trying to make. I told him that would be difficult for me because of my family history. But apparently this deal is going to be worth millions if not billions of dollars, and he's willing to throw in some things to make me more willing to go with him."

Rhea's jaw dropped in shock. "You're seriously thinking of going back to Argentina? Have you spoken to your mother about that?"

"No, I haven't. I'm an adult, and this is going to be a quick trip, two to three days at the most. I'm not planning to see my father."

"Your father hurt you and your mother. I don't think you should see him. He's not going to magically turn into a better person. He's still going to be the man who abandoned you. I hate to be blunt, but we both know that's true."

"But I don't know why he abandoned me. Mom doesn't ever want to talk about him, and you've never been forthcoming on the subject, either."

"It's your mom's story to tell—if she wants to tell it. You should talk to her."

"I plan on doing that, but I'm still going to make my own decision."

"I understand," Rhea said, not sounding too happy about it.

"Good, now getting back to the studio, can you give me a

week?"

"I'll think about it. I don't want to lose the offer I have. But I will talk to you before I make a final decision. I'm going to get some papers out of the office," Rhea said, vanishing down the hall.

Isabella glanced over at Ricardo. "I know you think I'm making a mistake."

"I think you're afraid," he said. "If you want to buy the studio, and you've found someone to give you the money, great. But you should still speak to the Tylers. Find out all your options, then make a decision. Otherwise, you're just running scared."

"I'm not scared. I know what I want."

"Then there's no danger in meeting with the Tylers. Tell them no to their faces. They gave you your first break on Broadway. Don't you owe them that?"

She let out a sigh as Ricardo's final point hammered home. Being loyal was one of her biggest faults. "I'll think about it."

Ricardo nodded with approval. "Good. But after you think about it—go down to the theater where they're holding auditions this week. Walk onto that stage and look into those lights and then tell me you don't want that anymore. Only then will I really believe you."

—⇒≫⋘⋞—

Isabella was still thinking about Ricardo's words when she went to the Grand View Towers Hotel a little before eight on Sunday night. In fact, she couldn't think about anything else, especially since she'd also gotten a long text on her phone from Donna Tyler expressing interest in having in their new show. She hadn't replied yet, because she didn't know what to say.

She'd really thought she was done with the stage, with performing, with chasing the Broadway dreams that had driven her life, but if she were going to consider going back, dancing for the Tylers would be the perfect scenario.

But even if she wanted to make another run at a starring role, could she do it? She'd definitely lost some of her muscle tone in the last year. She didn't work out the way she used to. She'd be winded in three minutes.

Frowning at that thought, she walked into the empty ballroom and told herself to focus on the present. Classes were starting in the morning and this was her new studio.

Nick's staff had done a great job. The hardwood floor was shined and polished. Mirrors had been set up all around the room, and two ballet barres had been installed along three of the walls. There was even a stereo system set up with speakers hung in the four corners of the room. It was perfect.

The door opened and Nick strode in. She liked the energy in his step. He didn't walk like he was going to the executioner as he'd done the first time he'd showed up for a lesson.

He'd finally put on some denim, but his dark gray jeans and maroon-colored shirt were probably as expensive as a three-piece suit. She couldn't help wondering if he ever wore ripped jeans or a sweatshirt. Maybe she just wanted him to look a little less attractive, less appealing, but that probably wouldn't happen even if he put on sweat pants and a wrinkled T-shirt. Nick had a masculine presence that would always draw a woman's eye.

"What do you think?" he asked. "Will the room work?"

"It's perfect. Thank you so much."

"You're welcome."

"Are you ready to dance?" She had a lot of things she wanted to talk to Nick about, but she also wanted to respect his lesson time. She'd agreed to teach him the tango. That had to come first.

He grimaced at her question. "I doubt I'll ever be ready, but let's get started. The sound system is set up for plug and play."

"I see that. Let's go over some of the steps first, then we'll put on the music."

"I thought you wanted me to concentrate more on the music than the steps," Nick countered.

"I'm changing it up a little. You have a very organized and practical mind, and I don't think you'll truly be able to relax and enjoy the music until you feel confident in your steps. So let's begin." She held out her hands to him.

As his fingers closed around hers, she had to fight back a little sigh of pleasure and concentrate on what she'd come here to do.

Twenty minutes later, Nick was able to put several combinations of steps together, so she turned on the music. The first few minutes were once again a disaster, mostly because Nick was rushing to be good, she realized. He didn't give himself time to learn. He wanted to be perfect as fast as possible. But he wasn't perfect, which led to frustration. She could see it in every tight determined line in his face.

She stopped the music. "This isn't a fight, Nick. There are no winners."

"Not true, Isabella. I dance this damned dance, and I win. I fall on my face, and I lose."

"I won't let you fall," she promised.

"I wish I could say the same. Your feet have already taken a beating."

"My feet are tough, and you won't drop me. I'm not at all worried about that."

"You should be."

"No." She shook her head and took both of his hands in hers as she gazed into his eyes. "When you hold me, I feel your strength. I know I can count on you. I want you to really lead this time. Take me where you want me to go."

Desire flashed through his eyes at her words, and she shivered. She was playing with fire, but Nick needed fire and passion. He was afraid to let it out, but if he didn't, he wouldn't succeed the way he wanted to.

"Okay," he said. "Let's do it again."

She turned on the music and moved back into his arms. "It's all you, Nick. I trust you."

"I'm going to try not to let you down."

"One-two-three," she began, and then Nick took the lead as she'd asked him to do. He still stumbled and hesitated every now and then, but she didn't try to take over. She let him continue and eventually he got better. By the time the dance was over, she didn't know who was more surprised— Nick or herself.

"That wasn't that bad," he muttered.

"Not bad at all. You just have to trust me as much as I trust you. That's what partnerships are all about. We have to play to our strengths and carry each other through the weak moments. That way at the end we're both still standing."

He gave her a thoughtful look as he considered her words. "You're not just talking about dancing, are you?"

"Of course I am." But what she'd said was true of all kinds of partnerships. "I think we're done for tonight. I hope you're feeling more optimistic."

"Actually, I am. Can we meet tomorrow?"

"I have back to back classes all day and night. Tuesday afternoon and Tuesday evening are free, though."

"Then we'll do it then. I'll check my schedule and get back to you on a time." Pausing, he added, "Can I buy you a drink in the bar?"

"That would be nice."

Nick turned off the lights as they left the ballroom, and

they walked down the stairs to the lobby bar. The lounge was fairly empty—only an older couple at one table and two younger men at another. Nick waved her toward a table by the fireplace, which gave off a warm, cozy heat. While it was almost summer, the day had been colder than yesterday, and the night had brought with it San Francisco's infamous fog bank.

The waitress gave them immediate attention, obviously knowing Nick was the owner. Their drinks arrived quickly along with a platter of cheeses, crackers and fruit that she didn't remember either of them ordering.

"I always eat well when I'm with you," she said lightly.

"I think the staff is trying to impress me," he returned. "But the food was a good call on their part. I worked up an appetite."

"Me, too." She spread some French Brie onto a cracker and popped it into her mouth. "Delicious."

"What did you do today?" Nick asked.

"I went to the studio for a few hours, met with some contractors and talked to my aunt."

"Is your aunt still planning to sell, or has her buyer disappeared?"

"She wants to sell now more than ever, and her buyer is apparently willing to take the studio over as is and do the repairs as long as the purchase price reflects the difference in money."

"They must really want the studio."

"I guess." She realized now that she should have asked Rhea more questions about the buyer. She should know who she was competing against. "You told me that you might be interested in investing. How serious were you about that?"

"I'm always serious about investments. What are you thinking?"

"That I would need a really big loan to match whatever

my aunt is being offered. I'm probably not a great risk. I don't have a lot of money in the bank. And I still don't know the extent of the water damage or how much it's going to cost to get the studio back into working condition."

"You just gave me a lot of reasons for why I shouldn't help you. That's not the way to make a sale."

"I don't want to lie to you. I can't even imagine why you would want to invest except that you really want me to go to Argentina, but if you're willing, I'd love to talk more about how we could set up a loan."

Nick stared back at her for a moment. "Do you have an accountant who does the studio books?"

"Yes. I can get you whatever financial information you need."

"I'll also need the estimates on the repair work and anything else you can tell me about how you envision your expenses going over the next one to two years."

"I can pull together everything I have, but I have to tell you that my aunt has given me maybe a week to match her offer, and I'm not sure I'll have that long."

"Drop off what you have tomorrow, and I'll take a look. I can't make a decision until I see the numbers."

"Completely understandable. I feel awkward and uncomfortable even asking you to do this, because it's a lot, and I know that it's probably more of a charity gesture than a sound business investment. I'm just feeling a little desperate."

"We'll talk more after I review the information."

"Okay, good," she blew out a breath. "So what did you do today?"

"I had some business to take care of."

"So no time for fun?"

"Not until now," he said with a smile.

"What do you do for fun when you're not working, if there's ever a moment when you're not focused on business?"

she asked curiously

He shrugged his shoulders. "The usual stuff. I read the paper, watch a ball game, work out."

"And see your friends?"

"Sure."

"Who are your close friends?"

"Martin is probably the closest to me. We've been working together for ten years."

"What about childhood friends or college pals?"

He shook his head. "I haven't kept up. I have no idea what anyone is doing."

"Then you must not be on social media," she said dryly. "I know the daily routines of people I haven't seen in fifteen years."

"You waste your time online?"

"Occasionally. I like seeing photos of my friends and keeping up with what's happening in their lives. But nothing takes the place of actually seeing them in person."

"You have a good group of friends." He leaned forward, resting his elbows on the table. "Who didn't I meet last night at the bowling alley?"

"Laurel. She's Andrea's twin sister. She got married last year and has been traveling a lot with her husband. You also didn't get to meet Maggie. She's the one who works at the Stratton, and the other missing person is Jessica. She and her son moved to San Diego last year, so lately the only times I've seen her have been at bridal events."

"So she was the first to get married?"

"Yes, but we weren't at her wedding. It was one of those spur-of-the-moment courthouse affairs, and it ended in divorce. That reaffirmed our promise to have big weddings with all of our friends together."

"You think a courthouse wedding is why she ended up divorced?"

"No, but I think the fact that they were in such a hurry and didn't really want to take the time to plan a wedding might have played a factor. However, I know that a big wedding doesn't guarantee a happy marriage."

"Sometimes a big wedding dooms the marriage. The groom realizes he just married a bridezilla."

She laughed. "Are you speaking from experience?"

"One of my friends married a very hyper, crazy girl who put him through hell during the wedding plans. I wasn't sure they were going to make it down the aisle. They did marry but were divorced three years later. I don't think the marriage ever lived up to the hype of the wedding—at least not in her mind."

"What kind of wedding would you want?" she asked curiously.

"I have no idea. Probably whatever my fiancé wanted."

"You'd let her call all the shots? That sounds a little risky."

"The risk would be in picking the right woman." He sipped his wine, then said, "What about you? What's your dream wedding?"

"Something small, intimate, outside, I think. I kind of picture myself barefoot on the beach, but that's probably not practical."

"It sounds nice, especially the small, intimate part of it."

"Well there will be seven bridesmaids," she added with a laugh. "So it won't be that small."

"I hope your groom has seven good friends."

"If he doesn't, I'm sure I can talk some of my bridesmaids into walking down the aisle with their husbands or boyfriends."

"You've got it covered."

"Except for the groom, it's all worked out," she said with a grin.

He smiled back. "I'm sure *Mr. Right* will come along."

"I'm not looking for *Mr. Right,* just the right man for me. But I'm not in a hurry. I have a lot of other things to worry about at the moment. In fact, I should probably get going. My first class tomorrow is at nine."

"I'll drive you home."

"No, this time I really insist on getting a cab. It's out of your way, and you're already doing so much for me."

"I'm getting something in return." He paused. "So we'll be leaving for Argentina on Friday."

Her gut clenched at the reminder that in a few short days she'd be heading back to the country where she'd been born. "Okay. And we'll be back on Monday?"

"If that's what you want. If you prefer to stay longer, that's fine, too. Have you given any thought about whether or not you want to contact your father while you're there?"

"I've given it some thought. I just haven't come to any conclusions."

"Well, you still have a few more days."

She might need a few more decades to make that decision. Unfortunately, she wasn't going to have that long.

Ten

Nick spent most of Monday trying not to go downstairs and see how Isabella's dance classes were going in the ballroom. He had far more pressing business to take care of, and if she were having any problems, she had his assistant's number and she could call for help, but she hadn't called. He hadn't heard a word from her since he'd put her in a cab the night before.

Getting up from his desk, he looked out the window. It was a cloudy day with a hint of rain in the forecast, and the unsettled sky matched his mood. Ever since Juan Carlos had asked him to dance the tango, his life had felt out of control. Actually, it wasn't just the contract amendment that had sent him spinning; it was Isabella. Maybe another teacher wouldn't have gotten him so stirred up. He might have been better able to concentrate on dancing rather than dreaming about kissing Isabella and taking her to bed.

But he didn't have another teacher, nor he did he want one. He liked Isabella. And while he didn't enjoy feeling like an awkward, clumsy person every time she turned on the music, he did enjoy being with her. Holding her, touching her, feeling her passion, even if it were only for the dance, was starting to be more enjoyable than he'd ever imagined. He almost didn't want it to end, but it would end. In less than a week, they'd go to Argentina. He'd perform the dance with

Isabella's help, and that would be it.

Or maybe not it. Isabella had emailed him some of the estimates for the studio repairs with a note that more information was coming.

Was he really going to invest in a run-down dance studio that would be managed by a woman who had absolutely no business experience and who had flat out told him she probably wasn't a great risk?

Of course he was, because it was Isabella who was asking for help, and how could he stand by and watch her lose her dream? He knew what it felt like to want something really badly. The land in Argentina had driven his every move since he was eighteen years old. He wanted that property as much as Isabella wanted her studio. And he could afford to help her, so why wouldn't he?

A knock came at his door. At his "come in," his assistant, Paula Rogers entered the room dressed in a black pencil skirt and silky gray blouse. At thirty-seven, Paula had been with him for eight years and was one of his most trusted employees. While he called her his assistant, she was in fact responsible for many of his ongoing projects, and when he'd received Isabella's studio information, he'd forwarded the numbers to her so that she could give him a preliminary report.

She set a file on his desk. "I printed everything out and attached my notes," Paula said. "I spoke briefly with Miss Martinez's accountant. He is going to forward some additional information later this afternoon."

"What are your notes going to tell me?" he asked.

"The return on investment will be very low if there is any return." She paused. "But I don't think your reasons for this particular investment have anything to do with profit potential, do they?"

"Not particularly," he admitted. "But I'd still like to know what I'm getting into. So take a look at the P&L when it comes in."

"I'll do that."

As Paula turned to leave, he added, "I'm going to step out for a while. I'll be back by four to meet with Martin." He grabbed his suit coat and headed out of the office and down to the Mezzanine level.

There were a couple of small children playing tag in the hallway outside the ballroom while a young woman who appeared to be a nanny texted on her phone. While it bothered him a little that the kids weren't being well supervised, he chose not to get worked up about it. The children would only be here for a few weeks, and he couldn't afford to do anything to upset Isabella before he got her on the plane to Argentina.

He opened the door to the ballroom and stepped inside. A class of young pre-teen girls were doing a routine under Isabella's instructions. They were really quite good, he thought. There was no playing around in this group. The atmosphere was serious and intense, and the couple of parents who sat on straight-back chairs at the other end of the room seemed completely immersed in what their children were doing.

Isabella wore leggings and a tank top that clung to every curve, and he found his mouth watering at the sight of her. Her hair was pulled back in a ponytail revealing a pair of silver hoop earrings hanging from her ears. She was pretty without even trying. She was also kind and encouraging to the girls, offering critical suggestions in a firm but cheerful voice. Isabella wasn't trying to tear anyone down but rather to build everyone up. It wasn't a coaching strategy he'd seen much of in his life. The guys he'd played baseball for had all been more comfortable with a shaming approach to coaching.

A woman came through the door and paused next to him—Isabella's aunt. "Mr. Hunter. I didn't expect to see you here."

"Just checking out how things were going."

"Could I have a word with you?"

"Sure."

"Isabella told me you're interested in buying the studio," Rhea said as they walked out of the ballroom.

"Yes. She's getting me the financials. I understand you have another interested buyer."

"I've received an excellent offer from a woman who has been part of the dance world for years. She's been on the East Coast but is expanding her operations to the West Coast. I understand her interest in my business; I don't understand yours."

Rhea's dark eyes were piercing, and he had a feeling she could see right through him. "My interest is in Isabella, in funding her dream," he said honestly. "She asked for my help, and I'd like to give it if I can."

"Obviously you can," Rhea said. "But the studio isn't Isabella's dream."

"I think you're wrong about that," he said slowly. "She's told me a number of times that the studio is her second home. It's her safe harbor."

"Exactly. It's her safe place; it's not her dream." Rhea paused. "Isabella is one of the most talented dancers I have ever seen, and I have seen a lot. I've been in her shoes. I know what it takes to the get to the top, and Isabella has it all: beauty, athleticism, grace, incredible feet and flexibility, and most of all, expression. She brings her emotions to every dance. She pours her heart out on the stage, and she is completely mesmerizing."

He swallowed hard at the images Rhea's words had created in his mind.

"But Isabella got hurt, not just physically but also emotionally. She came home to heal her broken bones and her broken heart. I was happy to have her in the studio, don't get me wrong, but I never wanted the studio to be the place where she hid out from life. It's the place you get prepared to launch into life."

"You want her to go back to the stage?"

"I do. She has a chance to audition for a musical that will open here in the city in a few months. The show is being produced by Hal and Donna Tyler, who are giants in the theater world. They love Isabella. They want her to be in their show, but she's afraid to go out for it. She hasn't danced on a stage since she had a horrible fall. I don't know if she told you about it."

"She mentioned it to me, but Isabella doesn't seem like the fearful type." He wondered if his assessment was off, or whether Rhea didn't know her niece as well as she thought she did.

"I don't know if it's some kind of post-traumatic stress, but Isabella is afraid to go back to chasing her dream. "I don't want my studio be a ball and chain holding Isabella to the ground when she was meant to fly. Life is about walking on the high wire. It's not about the net. Isabella is meant to be on that wire. It's who she is. If you're buying the studio because you care for her, then maybe you should reconsider. Do you really want to give her the net that will keep her trapped in a life that's only half of what it could be?"

He heard the passion in Rhea's voice. Whether she was wrong or right, she definitely cared a lot about Isabella. And he found himself wondering if he wasn't doing just what Rhea had said, giving Isabella a place to hide.

Was it any of his business that she was choosing to teach instead of to dance? Everyone would say no. And up until a few minutes ago, he would have said no, too.

But he did care about Isabella. He cared a lot. Maybe he needed to rethink how he could best help her get to where she needed to be.

"I'll think about what you've said," he told Rhea. "And then I'll talk to Isabella."

"That's all I ask. I hope you know that I have Isabella's best interests at heart. She comes across like someone who doesn't have a care in the world, but she's been hurt and now she's wary. I understand being cautious. But I also know that sometimes we all need a push to step outside of our comfort zones."

He'd certainly needed a push to get out of his comfort zone. If Juan Carlos hadn't inserted that damned clause in his contract, he'd be conducting business as usual instead of getting tangled up in the problems of one very beautiful and passionately artistic brunette.

Isabella finished her dance class and then walked over to her aunt who had taken a seat in the back of the room. She'd asked Rhea to meet her so they could go over the financial details she needed to send to Nick.

"Thanks for coming down," she said, taking a seat.

"Of course."

"Did I see you speaking to Nick?"

"We had a brief conversation," Rhea admitted. "I asked him why he was interested in my broken-down studio."

"What did he say?" Isabella asked.

"He said he wanted to help you fund your dream."

Her heart turned over at the words. "That was nice of him."

"He seems to be nice man. And he likes you—a lot. How do you feel about him? Is he just a student? A business partner? Or is there more between you?"

"I'm not really sure. I haven't known him very long."

"And yet he's already willing to put down quite a bit of cash to help you out."

"I don't think it's that much money where Nick is concerned." She paused. "Why does it matter to you where I get the money? You want out of the studio. I'm trying to find a way to make that happen while I can hang on to a place that means a lot to me."

"I just hate to see you settle, Isabella."

"I'm not settling. I'm making a realistic and practical decision."

"Exactly. Where is the passion, the heart?"

"It's in the studio," she retorted. "But I don't want to argue with you about it. I just need to provide Nick with our financial reports. Can you help me?"

Rhea pulled a thick manila envelope out of her bag. "The tax returns from the last two years are in here. I've also given the accountant permission to speak to Nick and his assistant."

"Thanks," she said. "What about the other buyer?"

"I've told her that I can let her know next Monday."

Isabella was relieved to have a few more days. "Who is the buyer?"

"Karen Halley."

"Of the Benton Hills Dance Academy?" she asked in surprise. "Why didn't you say that before?"

"You didn't ask. In fact, you didn't seem to want to know."

That was true. Not having a face to put on the unseen buyer had made that person seem less worrisome, but now that she knew it was Karen Halley who wanted the studio, she was definitely concerned.

"Karen has been wanting to open a West Coast studio for the last ten years," Rhea continued. "Having her out here would give our local dancers the opportunity to work under a first-class choreographer."

"And Karen would have access to a lot of extremely good talent," she murmured.

"It's a win-win," Rhea said.

"I'm sure Karen could find other space in the city."

"She's been looking for a while without much success." Rhea got to her feet. "I don't want to argue about it, Isabella. I need your offer by Monday. If you can't come up with the cash, I'm selling to Karen, because she's given me the same deadline. If I don't sell to her by then, the deal is off. I can't end up carrying this business anymore. Maybe that sounds cold to you, Isabella, but it's the way I feel."

"I understand. You've worked hard for a very long time." She stood up and gave her aunt a hug. "I don't want this studio to come between us. I love you. We're family."

"And family should look out for one another," Rhea said. "I'm not convinced that selling you the studio is in your best interests."

"I think I'm old enough to make that decision."

Rhea smiled. "Sometimes I still think you're twelve years old."

"But I'm not."

"No, you're not. Let me know if you need anything else, Isabella."

"Thanks. It's all going to work out the way it's supposed to."

"I hope so," Rhea returned. "The studio has always been the place where dreams are born. I just don't want it to be the place where dreams die."

And with those ominous words, Rhea left the ballroom.

Isabella sat back down for a long minute, trying to shake off the bad feeling that had come over her with Rhea's parting statement. She knew what she wanted. She couldn't let her aunt's doubts change her mind—could she?

Shaking her head, she got to her feet and told the

assistant dance instructor she'd be back in a few minutes. Then she headed to the elevator. She still had the card key for the fifteenth floor and soon she was approaching the desk of Nick's assistant, Paula.

"Is Nick by chance available?" Isabella asked. "I wanted to drop off some tax information."

"I'm sorry, but he's in a meeting," Paula said.

She knew that was true because she could see Nick in the glass-walled conference room. He stood at the end of a long table, and seated around that table were at least fifteen people, reminding Isabella that Nick ran a huge company.

Why on earth would he want to invest in her studio, in her problems? He didn't care about dance at all. He was just doing it to make sure she got on that plane for Argentina.

Well, that was his choice. She wasn't going to feel guilty about it. She wasn't twisting his arm.

"If you'd like to leave your information, I'll make sure Mr. Hunter gets it," Paula said.

Isabella handed over the thick envelope. "Thanks. I'd appreciate it."

"No problem. I know he's eager to see the entire financial picture."

Isabella had a feeling Nick's eagerness would wane when he saw the actual figures. But for now she was going to keep pressing forward.

Tuesday morning Isabella was back in the ballroom teaching classes, talking to students, and checking her phone every five minutes to see if Nick had left her a message or a text, but she hadn't heard a word from him since she'd dropped off the tax information Monday afternoon. It hadn't been that long, but the clock was ticking, and she needed answers.

When her lunchtime class ended, she checked her phone again. There was no message from Nick, but there were two texts from the Tylers and one from Ricardo, all asking her to come down to the theater and talk about the new production. There was a small part of her that was tempted to go, but there was another part of her that told her not to weaken, not to give in. She had a life now, and it was good. She needed to stay focused on things she could control, and having the opportunity to dance on a stage and be part of a production was something she couldn't control. She'd given her heart and her soul to the stage, and she'd been crushed in more ways than one. She was better off now. She just needed to stay the course.

Glancing at the calendar on her phone, she realized she had three free hours before her next class. She was debating what she wanted to do with that time when Nick walked through the door, and her heart skipped a beat in what was becoming a very familiar jolt of attraction.

"Isabella, I heard you might have a few hours free," he said.

"Who told you that?"

"I stopped by the studio earlier this morning. I wanted to take a look at the damage for myself."

"You should have told me. I would have gone with you."

"It was an impulsive decision."

She raised an eyebrow at that. "You don't make impulsive decisions, remember?"

"You seem to be rubbing off on me."

"So what did you think?" she asked, pretty sure she wouldn't like his answer.

"It's all fixable with time and money."

Well, that didn't sound too bad, nor did Nick look particularly discouraged, another good sign.

"I want to talk to you more about it," he continued. "Ricardo mentioned to me that you had some free time this afternoon."

"That's true," she said, a little relieved that she would be too busy to even consider calling the Tylers back.

"Can I steal you away?"

"Sure." She walked over to the chair and grabbed her bag and then followed him out to the lobby. His car was with the valet, and he quickly ushered her inside. "Are we going to lunch?" she asked.

"Eventually," he replied. "I need to make a stop first. There's something I want you to see."

"Sounds good. Did you get a chance to read through the information I left with Paula?" she asked as he drove away from the hotel.

"I did. It made for some very interesting bedtime reading."

"Put you right to sleep, did it?"

He smiled. "Not at all. I actually enjoy reading financial reports. They provide an excellent snapshot of a company, but unfortunately they don't tell the whole story."

"If you're missing something you need, tell me what it is, and I'll get it for you. I want you to have all the facts so you can make a good decision."

"I'm glad you feel that way, because I don't make any decision without having all the facts."

"So what do you need?"

"You'll see."

She didn't care for his answer, but it was clear he wasn't going to tell her more at the moment.

Her uneasiness increased when Nick turned into a parking garage just off Market. "Where are we going?"

He repeated his earlier answer, "You'll see."

"You're being mysterious."

"And you're worrying a little too much for a free-spirited woman who likes to go with the flow."

"I'm not as free-spirited as I used to be."

"I'm beginning to realize that," he said as they exited the car and walked out of the garage.

When they turned down the next street, she saw the front of the Orpheum Theater, and her pulse jumped. The Tylers were holding auditions at the Orpheum all week. Nick had talked to Ricardo earlier and Rhea yesterday.

She stopped abruptly. "What's going on, Nick?"

"You have some people you need to talk to. They're waiting for you inside."

"You set up a meeting with the Tylers?" The idea seemed incredible. A wave of anger ran through her.

"Ricardo set it up. I just agreed to get you here."

"How dare you try to control my life? How would you like it if I butted into your business?"

"I wouldn't like it at all," he said evenly. "But you told me that I was entitled to all the information I needed to make a good decision about the studio. That information includes whether or not I'll be investing in someone whose career is meant to be somewhere besides a dance studio."

She looked at him in astonishment. "The dance studio is where I'm meant to be."

"Is it? Would you be there now if you hadn't gotten injured or hurt by the man you loved?"

"Yes. No. I don't know," she said, waving her hand in frustration. "But both those things happened, and I am where I am."

"Because you're afraid."

"What do you know about it?"

"I know that your aunt thinks you should be dancing, that you have a special gift, and that she doesn't want the studio to be an excuse or a hideout. I know that Ricardo agrees with her, and they appear to be the two people in your life who know you the best."

"Apparently, they don't know me at all," she said with annoyance.

"So prove them wrong. Walk into the theater, meet with the producers, and then make a decision."

"I've already made a decision."

"Then you have nothing to be afraid of. If it's the right decision, no one will be able to change your mind." He held her gaze for a long minute. "What's it going to be, Isabella?"

"You're not going to give me the money if I don't go inside, are you?"

"I don't know. What happens in the next minute is going to tell me a lot about you."

"Fine. I'll go inside, but in case you were wondering…I hate you a little bit right now."

"Good to know."

Eleven

Isabella drew in a deep breath as she turned toward the theater. It was not a big deal, she told herself. She wasn't going to audition or take the stage. She was just going to meet with the Tylers, thank them for their interest, and say goodbye.

But as she stepped through the theater doors, she felt like she was stepping back in time. She could remember the first time she'd gone to a musical. She'd been nine years old, and she'd fallen in love with the show, the actors, the music—everything. She'd wanted to be one of those dancers on the stage. She'd wanted to play a character and take the audience with her on a dramatic journey through dance and song.

From that day forward, she'd spent all of her time preparing herself to be that performer. She'd played in her high school and college musicals, performed at dance competitions and gotten bit parts in shows in her early twenties. And then she'd made it to the big time, to Broadway, to a show that would actually open on the famed street.

It had all gone to hell.

The pain of those memories made her feel sick. She might have turned and run if she hadn't felt Nick's strong presence behind her. She couldn't let him be right. She couldn't be afraid to be in a place that had once meant so much to her.

She forced herself to move through the lobby and into the darkened theater. She'd barely made it to the third to last row when she heard her name ring out.

"Isabella?"

It was Donna walking down the aisle to greet her. Tall, blonde and thin, Donna was a beautiful forty-six-year-old woman with some of the best choreographic instincts in the business. Her husband Hal was in his early fifties and still had the good looks of the leading man he had once been. Now he was all about business and money. In some ways, Hal reminded her of Nick.

Donna threw her arms around Isabella, pulling her into a tight hug. "I'm so glad you came. When Ricardo called, he said he wasn't sure you would show up, but he was hopeful. I was hopeful, too."

Seeing the genuine warmth in Donna's eyes, Isabella felt a little guilty for not having called her back.

"We've been running through dance auditions all day," Donna continued. "We want to show you a number we've been working on and get your opinion. Come and say hello to Hal and the others." Donna paused, looking past Isabella to Nick. "I'm sorry. I was so caught up in seeing Isabella I didn't realize she'd come with someone."

"This is Nick Hunter," Isabella said. "And this is Donna Tyler, one of the producers of this new show."

"Don't mind me," Nick said after greeting Donna. "I'm just here as Isabella's driver."

Isabella rolled her eyes at that. "Don't believe him for a second. Nick is a very successful businessman."

"Well, we always like to meet successful businessmen," Donna said. "We can never have too many investors. Anyway, come on down you two."

They followed Donna down the aisle. Soon Isabella

found herself being hugged by Hal, the Tylers' assistant, Mary Donohue, and a choreographer she'd worked with before, Malcolm Hodges. The director, a man by the name of James Bennett, was the only one she hadn't met previously."

"I've heard many good things about you, Isabella," James said, giving her a speculative look. "Donna tells me you're the best dancer she's ever worked with."

"She was exaggerating."

"I wasn't," Donna denied. "I was telling the truth. I'm just sorry that you got hurt on our show. That should have never happened."

"We don't need to talk about that."

"Good, because we want to talk about this show," Donna said. "Malcolm, what do you think about showing Isabella our opening number?"

"Excellent idea. But I'm going to need some help." He extended his hand. "Come on stage with me, Isabella."

"I'm not prepared to dance."

"You're dressed for it," Malcolm said.

"Well, I was teaching, but I haven't warmed up or anything."

"I just want to show you some steps. No backflips or anything," he joked.

She drew in a much-needed breath, feeling like this meeting was getting away from her. There were a lot of curious gazes on her, and while she couldn't see Nick, she knew he was waiting for her answer, too. Would she be afraid to go back on the stage? Or would she be brave?

"All right," she said, before she could change her mind. "Let's see this dance."

--➤➤◄◄◄--

As she climbed the steps to the stage, she felt a wave of

fear run through her. Her stomach tightened and churned. Her head felt tight and full as if any movement would make her dizzy, make her fall. But she wasn't going to fall. She wasn't climbing up a ladder. She wasn't going to be attached to a harness and dropped onto the stage; she was just walking.

She barely heard what Malcolm had to say for the first five minutes. Her brain was completely scattered, moments from the past flashing through her head. When she looked to the wings, she was assailed with memories, most of them happy. How excited she'd been to wait for her cue, to come onto the stage and perform the way she'd always dreamed of performing.

When she looked out to the theater, to the empty seats, she remembered those seats being filled with people during their early workshop performances. She could hear the hush when the emotions on the stage got heavy and then the surge of applause at the high points, the endless clapping for an encore. She'd thought then that the show would run for years. It would be one of those Broadway classics that never died.

But they hadn't made it out of the pre-opening shows before disaster had struck. When she'd fallen, everything else had come crashing to the ground as well. It hadn't been her fault. Logically she knew that—despite the fact that Carter had tried to pin it on her. He'd pushed too hard, taken shortcuts, and that's why the dream had been destroyed.

She realized now that the dream was still there. It was just a different dream, maybe one she could live out again—if she wanted to…

"I want to show you the first combination of steps," Malcolm told her, putting his hand on her arm. He gazed into her eyes. "Will you do them with me, Isabella?"

It was such a simple question to shoot so many complicated emotions through her body. In the end, she made the answer simple, too. "Yes."

———⇥⇤———

Nick sat up straighter in his seat as Isabella and the choreographer began to walk through some steps. He'd been thrilled to see her up on the stage, but watching the expressions that had moved through her eyes and across her face for the last five minutes, he'd started to wonder if he'd done the right thing in bringing her here. He'd ambushed her. He'd gone against her wishes and sided with her aunt and her friend.

And he didn't even know why he'd done it, why he'd gotten involved at all.

Actually, that wasn't true. It was because of her. And it wasn't because he wanted to protect his money and that he needed to know if she was done with performing so that he could be certain she would manage the dance studio efficiently. It wasn't that at all. It was hearing Rhea and Ricardo talk about how Isabella was meant to perform but was afraid to go back that had made him want to give her a nudge or a shove or whatever you wanted to call it.

She'd already told him she hated him a little for it, but now that she was working with the choreographer, he had new hope. She moved as stiffly as he'd ever seen her. In fact, watching her now made him think that's probably what he looked like when she tried to teach him the tango.

The stiffness came from fear.

Isabella was afraid to embrace the life she'd had and lost. And he was afraid to look foolish, to look less than he was. He'd always tried to present himself in a certain way, cool, controlled, smart and sophisticated. It was a persona that worked well in business but not as well on the dance floor.

Did he really need that persona anymore? He'd achieved a lot, more than even he had imagined when he'd first started out. Had he lost his true self somewhere along the way?

Had Isabella done the same thing? She was dead set on being a dance teacher, a studio owner, protecting and keeping the place she'd always called home. But wasn't her life really somewhere else? Wasn't it in a theater like this one?

The questions rolled around in his head. At least one of the answers became clearer when Malcolm put on some music, and he and Isabella performed a short combination of steps.

With every spin, every twirl, every look, Isabella set the stage on fire. She was a natural performer. She drew the audience in, and held them there until the story was told and the dance was done. The other conversations going on in the theater faded away as she danced. And when she looked out towards the audience, he thought she was dancing just for him.

His heart flipped over at the thought. He couldn't help wondering if he hadn't made a big mistake bringing her here. He'd forced her to see what she was giving up. If she did go back to the theater, they would probably never see her again. If they were partners in her studio, they'd have to have contact.

But even if she stayed at the studio and he invested, what would come next?

They didn't go together. She was a dancer, an artist, emotional and passionate and a magnet for trouble. He was a businessman—determined, ruthless, pragmatic about life—and he hated trouble. But he didn't hate Isabella. He wished he could.

Applause rang through the theater as Malcolm and Isabella finished their impromptu dance.

Isabella came down from the stage to be greeted with more enthusiasm from the Tylers. They wanted her to come back. They wanted her to be their star. They wanted her to have everything she'd never thought she could have again.

It was going to be very difficult for her to say no. But she did manage to put them off, saying she needed to think it over.

He got to his feet as she came back up the aisle.

"I should kill you," she said.

He was happy that her expression of joy didn't match her words. "You liked it up there."

"Which is why I'm not killing you. Let's get out of here."

Isabella didn't say another word until they left the theater. Then she stopped in the middle of the sidewalk and said, "I still can't believe you tricked me into coming here."

"I can't believe you didn't come on your own. When you danced on the stage, I saw the real you—or the *you* that you should be. You don't want to teach right now, Isabella. Maybe that's later, when you're older, when you have a few more stories to tell, but not now."

"I thought I was done, Nick."

"How could you be when you didn't make the choice—it was made for you? But your injury has healed. And you have another chance. Why wouldn't you take it?"

"I don't think I'm as good as I used to be. I was dancing five to seven hours a day when I was working on Broadway. I've slacked off. I'm older. Do you know how many fantastic nineteen-year-olds there are? The Tylers could easily get someone in better shape with fantastic technique."

"But they clearly want you. Why is that?"

"Maybe it's guilt. Maybe they thought they were partially responsible for my accident."

"If that were the case, they would have made one call, and when you said no, that would have been the end of it. But that wasn't the case."

"That's true. They do seem to genuinely want me."

"It looked that way to me. Everyone thinks you're great.

Apparently, the only person you have left to convince is yourself. When did you stop believing in your talent?"

"I don't know. Maybe about the time I fell to the stage."

"I know you got hurt, not just physically but emotionally. But you got back up on the stage today and you shined like the star that you are."

She looked up at him with her dark brown eyes framed by ridiculously long lashes, and his gut clenched at her beauty. He'd probably just gotten her started on a life of rehearsals and shows and traveling around the world. He'd basically done everything he could to make sure they never saw each other again. What the hell was wrong with him?

"Thank you," she said. Then she shocked him by flinging her arms around his neck and pulling his head down to hers.

He didn't know if it was a kiss of gratitude or what, but he didn't care. It had been too long since he'd had her mouth under his.

Isabella kissed with her heart and her soul, holding nothing back, which made him want to hold nothing back, which was a slightly terrifying thought. Because he always held back, analyzed every situation and carefully plotted out his moves and his relationships.

But kissing Isabella was a little like jumping off a cliff. He had no idea where he'd land, but it would be a hell of a ride.

Unfortunately, that ride was shortened by the heckling noises of a couple of teenagers walking by.

Isabella stepped back with a slightly embarrassed smile. "I guess I got a little carried away."

"I like when you get carried away."

"I could say the same for you, Nick. It's nice when you let down your guard, which doesn't happen that often." She pulled out her phone as it began to buzz. "Ricardo again. I have five messages all wanting to know how I'm doing, what

I'm thinking, and if I'm going to strangle him for telling you about the Tylers' show."

"Are you going to answer him?"

"I'll let him sweat it out for a bit. But I do need to get back to work. I have a class in half an hour. I didn't realize how long we were in the theater."

"Let's get back to the car."

"So what did you think of the dance number?"

"I'm no expert, but I thought it was very clever and entertaining. You were amazingly good for just being thrown into a new dance."

"The steps were familiar to me. I've been dancing so long, it's more about changing up the order and adding variations than learning completely new steps. I did like Malcolm's ideas. He's one of the most creative and challenging choreographers working in dance today."

"What is the show about?"

"A girl who goes to New York to make it on the stage."

He smiled at the description. "Sounds like a part that was written for you."

"Or for any dancer who has dreamed of performing on the most important stage in the world. Donna and Hal are very good at creating storylines filled with emotion and drama. The characters, dialogue, dance and music create an experience that audiences love. They're a great team."

"So why are you hesitating, Isabella? Why wouldn't you want to work with them? Why didn't you just say yes?"

"The studio. My aunt is going to sell it, and if I don't buy it now, I'll never have the chance again."

"You might have another shot at it down the road. Or you might find you want to build your own studio from the ground up, when you're really ready, not just because your aunt is ready."

"I have some things to think about."

"Yes, you do," he said as he opened the car door for her.

"Nick," Isabella said. "Thanks for butting into my business. If I can ever return the favor, let me know."

"Actually," he began.

She raised an eyebrow. "Really? You're inviting me to butt into your business?"

"No, I'm inviting you to dinner tomorrow night with my father. It's his birthday, and I've been ordered to make an appearance. I'd rather not go alone."

Surprise moved through her dark eyes. "You want me to meet your dad?"

"I could use a buffer, and my father is always distracted by a beautiful woman."

"A distracting buffer, huh?" she said with a nod. "Okay, I can do that. Do you think your father will like me?"

"Sure," he said, but as he closed the door he thought that his father would probably hate Isabella, especially as his date. His father had dangled heiresses and up-and-coming young lawyers in front of him the past few years. Most of those women had either been on his dad's payroll or had a reason to keep his father happy by spying on him. But Isabella was his—all his.

Well, at least for a few more days...

Twelve

—➤ ➤➤ ◄◄ ◄—

Isabella finished off the day's dance classes a little after seven. When the last students left the ballroom, her aunt walked into the room, a wary expression on her face.

"You should be scared to talk to me," Isabella told her.

Rhea offered an apologetic look. "I know it was shady, but when Ricardo told me about the Tylers and their new show, I really wanted you to audition. So did Ricardo."

"So you coerced Nick into tricking me into going down there with him?"

He didn't take a lot of coercion. Nick doesn't want to invest in the studio if it's not going to be the business you really want to run."

"The only reason he has doubts about whether or not I want to run the dance studio is because of you and Ricardo. You two had no business going behind my back."

"We love you. We want the best for you."

"I'm a grown woman. I can make my own decisions."

"You were making the wrong decision because you were scared. I couldn't stand by and do nothing. What kind of aunt would I be?"

"I can't help thinking your motivation was not as selfless as you're making it out to be. You want to sell the studio to Karen Halley."

"I think Karen will do wonderful things with the business

I've created," Rhea admitted. "Karen has also thought long and hard about opening a West Coast studio. She's ready. I don't think you've had the same amount of time to really consider all your options. That's partly my fault, because Karen's offer came in, and then the plumbing broke. But we are where we are. I want you to be happy Isabella, and if I truly believed that running my studio would be your dream job, then I'd send Karen packing. But I just don't believe that this is the right time for you."

"Again, it's my decision."

"Have you made a decision? How was your meeting with the Tylers?"

She hated to say it went well, because it would just prove her aunt right, but she also didn't want to lie. "It was all right."

"Just all right?" her aunt said with disappointment.

"Fine. It was good. It was fun to see them again, to hear about their production, and to be wanted."

"They offered you a part, didn't they?"

"I told them I'd think about it."

"Is there really anything to think about?"

"I have moved on, going from a dancer to a teacher, and I like teaching, watching the younger dancers find their feet."

"But…"

"But it felt amazing to be on the stage again," she admitted.

"Honey, you can always teach. Maybe not for my studio, but you can open your own place one day. You only have a few more years left to be the dancer you always wanted to be. Don't waste them."

"I need to think about it. You offered me until Monday. Is that still good?"

"Of course," she said, frustration still evident in her voice. "But no longer than that."

"I understand."

"Can I buy you dinner?" Rhea asked as Isabella gathered up her things.

"No thanks. I'm going to stop by Mom's house."

"Will you tell her about Argentina?"

"I will."

"Then you're definitely going?"

"Yes. It seems to be a week of big decisions for me. One down, two to go."

Looking at her mother, Kathleen, was a little like looking in a mirror, Isabella thought as her mom opened the door of her condo with a happy smile. Her mom had dark brown hair and brown eyes and they shared the same nose. The only think Isabella had really gotten from her father was his olive skin.

"You're here. I can't believe I haven't seen you in almost three weeks," Kathleen said, giving her a loving hug.

"It's been crazy busy," she said, following her mother into her home.

"Rhea told me about the plumbing issues. I offered a small loan, but she said the problem was too big for a Band-Aid."

"That's true." She took a seat on the sofa in the living room.

"What can I get you to drink, honey?"

"Nothing. I'm fine for now. What smells so good?"

"Vegetarian lasagna. It's almost ready." Kathleen sat down on the couch next to her. "Bill and I have been traveling so much the past year that I feel like I'm never at home to cook."

"How is Bill?" she asked, wondering if her mother's

long-term boyfriend would join them for dinner. Kathleen and Bill Webber had been going out for almost eight years, but they still kept their own condos and didn't seem in any hurry to make a long-term commitment to each other. That didn't surprise Isabella. Her mother's divorce from her father had been so painfully brutal that it seemed to have put her mom off marriage entirely.

"He's well. He's in Chicago this week visiting his sister and her family."

"You didn't want to go with him?"

"Actually, I was happy to have some alone time. I love that man, but he adores being on the go, and sometimes I like to just be quiet. Plus, I haven't seen you in a while. What's new? Besides the studio plumbing problems?"

"I'm giving tango lessons to Nick Hunter, the owner of the Grand View Towers Hotel. He's also letting us use a portion of the ballroom for our dance classes while repairs are being made."

"Rhea told me about the ballroom but not about the tango lessons."

"Nicks needs to learn to dance the tango for a business deal. His company is trying to buy a beautiful piece of coastal property in Argentina. In order to seal the deal he has to dance the tango for the seller."

Her mother stiffened at the mere mention of Argentina. Isabella drew in a deep breath, knowing there would be no better time to tell her mother about her trip.

"Nick asked me to go with him to Argentina to perform the dance as his partner. I've agreed to go."

Her mother's face paled. "Are you serious? You're going to see your father?"

"No, I'm going to Argentina to dance the tango."

"Then you won't look your dad up?"

"I don't know," she said honestly. "I'm torn. I wanted to

talk to you about it."

"The man lost all rights to your love and attention a very long time ago, Isabella. Why would you want to see him now?"

"I'm curious. I don't understand why he stopped talking to me. The last time I saw him was my eighth-grade graduation, and whenever I tried to talk to you about him, she shut me down. You never wanted to talk about him, to explain his behavior."

"There was no explanation, and I told you many times that he had problems."

"Yes, you hinted at some issues, but you always clammed up when I asked questions."

"It was painful to talk about him," her mother admitted. "And I didn't want you to look back, only forward. I tried to make up for his absence, to make sure that you had everything you needed."

"I did have what I needed," she reassured her mother. "You were always there for me, and that's why I never tried to contact him. I didn't want to be disloyal to you, to make you feel like you weren't enough. But I've always had questions. He is my father. I have a biological connection to the man."

"That's all you have." Kathleen stared back at her through angry, dark eyes. Her lips were set in a tight, tense line. Finally, she continued. "When I met your father, I thought he was the most wonderful man in the world. He was warm and outgoing, everyone's friend. He was doing well in his job as a diplomat. He was very sophisticated and cosmopolitan. He swept me off my feet. It wasn't until you were two or three years old that I began to realize that his partying lifestyle was out of control. And when your father drank, he got mean. He would say terrible things to me and to you, and then the next morning he would forget what he'd said. But I couldn't forget how hateful he'd been."

Her mother paused, then went on. "I asked him to get help, and he said he would stop drinking, but while he'd be good for a few weeks, something would always happen. Sometimes when he drank, he also took drugs. It was part of his social scene. But I wasn't in that scene. I was at home with a small child and worried that my husband wasn't going to be able to provide for me. As his problems increased, he started having trouble at work. Finally, it all came to a head. He lost his job, and he went completely out of control. I tried to hang on to the marriage, but I couldn't. Finally, I said I was leaving. He was drunk at the time. He said he was happy I was going, that I'd made his life hell and that he didn't think you were even his daughter. He accused me of cheating on him with one of his friends. I didn't cheat, Isabella. You are his daughter."

She nodded slowly, feeling a little sick to her stomach that her father would have tried to disown her in such a way. She was beginning to feel sorry she'd pressed her mother to finally explain what had happened. But while her mother had been reluctant to start talking, there seemed to be no stopping her now.

"Your father came to the States a year later," Kathleen said. "He told me that he'd cleaned up his act and gotten sober. I wanted to believe him. I let you see him. I let him write to you. And I had some hope that maybe he could turn his life around. I wanted him to be well, to be the man I'd fallen in love with and had a child with. But when he came to your eighth-grade graduation four years later, I saw that he was slipping back into the old ways. Later that year, I heard from his sister that he'd gotten into legal trouble and had been arrested. He ended up going to jail for embezzling money from his employer."

"What?" she asked in astonishment. "You never told me that."

"I thought it was best that you just think he was a neglectful father, not a criminal. I also believed it was even more important at that point to keep the two of you apart."

"I don't understand how you could keep something like that from me. Is that why he didn't write to me, because he couldn't?"

"No," her mother said quickly. "He had access to mail. I think he was probably embarrassed to write you while he was in jail."

"How long was he there?"

"I think it was three or four years."

Isabella studied her mother's face. There was something she wasn't telling her. "Did you hear from him while he was in jail?"

"I heard from him about a year before he got out. He told me that he'd had time to reflect on everything he'd done and he was sober and he was going to start over."

"Did you answer him?"

"No, I didn't," her mom said flatly. "I was done. Maybe you can't understand that. Perhaps it seems harsh to you, but I had wasted too many years worrying about that man and trying to fix him for you. I couldn't do it anymore."

"Was that the last time you heard from him?"

"Yes."

"So that was how long ago?"

Her mother sighed. "About seven years I would say."

She silently did the math. "Then he was in jail while I was in high school and my first two years of college."

"Does it really matter, Isabella?" her mother asked wearily. "Do you think seeing him now would change anything for you?"

"He might have gotten his life together."

"I hope he did. I don't wish bad things for him—at least not anymore. But he hasn't contacted me, nor has he reached out to you. Everyone has moved on, Isabella. You're not going to suddenly get the father you never had. That man doesn't exist. I honestly believe that trying to see him will only hurt you."

Her mother's passionate words rang through her head. She didn't want to get hurt again, but she might have to take the risk.

"I want you to know that I've heard everything you've said, and I really appreciate your finally telling me the whole truth." She paused. "That was the whole truth, wasn't it?"

Her mother nodded. "Yes, it was."

"You mentioned before that you'd heard from Dad's sister that he was in jail. Do you still keep in touch with her?"

"No, I don't. Carlotta wanted me to write to him, and I refused. That was the end of our relationship. His family always felt like I didn't do enough to keep him happy, as if it were my fault that he drank too much. I think they were in as much denial as he was."

"They must have been, because Dad's drinking was not your fault. You were an incredible mother to me. You worked two jobs to give me a good life. I need you to know that I know that. Whatever Dad's family had to say means nothing, because I was there. I saw what you did for me."

Her mother's eyes filled with moisture. "It's what mothers do for their children. My jobs sometimes got in the way of us being close, but I felt it was important to give you a stable home. I didn't want you to lack for anything because your parents were no longer married. Thankfully, Rhea picked up the slack. You two had so many interests in common. Sometimes I felt a little jealous, but mostly I was relieved to have the help."

"I was lucky to have both you and Aunt Rhea. I am going to Argentina, because I promised Nick that I would, and he's doing a lot for me in return. I don't know if I'm going to look

Dad up or not. At this point, I doubt it, but to be completely honest, I probably won't decide until I get there."

"You're an adult now. You can do what you want. Just promise me one thing…"

"What's that?"

"If you do see him, don't let your father try to rewrite history with his charming smile. You always like to think the best of people, even when they don't deserve it."

"I like to give people a chance to be good, but I'm not a fool. I know what's true and what's not."

"I hope so. You have a big heart. That makes me proud but also makes me worry."

"Well, right now all you have to worry about is feeding me. Time for lasagna?"

"Absolutely," her mom said, getting to her feet, relief in her eyes that their painful discussion was now over.

"Great. I missed lunch, so I'm starving." She followed her mom into the kitchen.

"While we're eating, you can tell me what else is new. Did I hear something about you trying out for a new musical?"

She groaned. "Rhea has a big mouth."

Her mother laughed. "Of course she does. So are you thinking of going back on the stage?"

"Maybe, but if you don't mind, I'd rather not talk about it tonight."

"That's fine. In that case you can tell me what is really going on between you and Nicholas Hunter," her mother said with a knowing gleam in her eye.

"I told you. We're dancing the tango together."

"Is that *all* you're doing together?"

"Not exactly," she admitted. "There is something between us, but it can't go anywhere."

"Why not?" her mom asked as she pulled the lasagna out

of the oven and set it on the stove.

"We're very different people, and we don't want the same things in life."

"Wanting different things from life is okay as long as you also want each other. Maybe you could complement each other."

"Or we could drive each other crazy," she said with a laugh. "Nick is very complicated. He's hard to get to know and he's carrying some baggage from the past that I don't completely understand. But I know there are family issues."

"You can relate to family issues."

She nodded. "True. Nick's parents didn't divorce, but I think they were unhappy for a while. Nick's mom died when he was about eighteen, and he doesn't seem to have much of a relationship with his father, although I may learn more about that tomorrow night.

"What's tomorrow night?"

"Nick is taking me to his dad's birthday party."

Her mother raised an eyebrow. "Nick is introducing you to his father?"

"Don't get too excited. He basically said he'd like me to be a buffer between him and his dad."

"Oh, honey," her mom said with a laugh. "You're lying to yourself if you think all you are is a buffer. The man likes you and you like him. The real question is—what are you going to do about it?"

"That is the question," she agreed. "I just wish I had an answer."

Thirteen

Nick felt remarkably tense as he double-parked in front of Isabella's apartment building just before seven on Wednesday night. It wasn't just his father's upcoming birthday party that bothered him; it was also Isabella. He couldn't seem to stop thinking about her. He'd never felt so distracted or unfocused.

After his mother died, he'd always had goals, things he needed to achieve for her and for himself. He'd had a plan, a purpose, and he'd gone full steam ahead toward that purpose every day of his life until the past week.

Now, he found himself humming Latin tunes, subconsciously tapping out steps in the elevator, thinking about kissing Isabella, running his fingers through her hair, taking off her clothes, seeing every naked inch of her beautiful, graceful, athletic body.

Damn! He shifted in his seat as his thoughts made him once again uncomfortable.

What the hell was wrong with him? He didn't get this worked up about a woman. Or if he did get worked up, he worked it out in bed fairly quickly. But that wasn't an option with Isabella, at least not right now. He needed to get her to Argentina, dance the tango, and then decide whether or not he could risk screwing things up with probably the most fantastic sex he would ever have.

Isabella opened the car door and gave him the smile that

jump-started his heart every single time.

"Sorry to keep you waiting," she said. "As you've probably guessed by now, I tend to run a little late. I'm always trying to squeeze in one more thing."

"It's fine. I'm not in a hurry to get to my father's place." In fact, he didn't know why he'd given in to his father's demand that he show up for his birthday. It wasn't like they had any kind of a real father-son relationship, so why even pretend they did? But he knew the answer why—because his father liked his friends to think he'd done well as a father and a family man, not just as a businessman. It wouldn't look good if his son didn't show up for his birthday.

"Tell me about your dad," Isabella said as they headed across town.

"What do you want to know?"

"What's he like?"

He tried to think of the right words to describe his father. "He's tall."

"That's it?" she asked. "Come on, Nick, you can do better than that."

"He is really tall—six foot six. He's always used his height to intimidate people."

"Okay, he's tall," she said with a little laugh. "What else?"

"He can be charming, smooth. Women usually like him. He loves golf. He makes more deals on the golf course than he does in the office."

"Do you play?"

"Once in a while. It's not really my game."

"Because it's your father's game?"

Isabella was very perceptive, something that he both liked and disliked, because she seemed to read him better than most people. "That's part of it," he admitted. "But mostly it's because it's slow. I'd rather play basketball or bike."

"Do you bike in the gym or outside?"

"Both." He shot her a quick look. "Do you like to ride?"

"I did a lot of spin classes when I was rehabbing my leg, but I didn't ride outside. Too much traffic in the city."

"There are some great rides outside of the city and down the coast."

"That would be more fun. I don't like having to worry about cars. I get distracted very easily by pretty scenery," she added with a self-deprecating smile.

And if he biked behind her, there was no doubt he'd be watching her instead of the road. "You should probably stay away from city streets then."

"Exactly."

"Your dad lives here?" she asked as he turned into an underground parking garage for a very tall building near downtown.

"Forty-eighth floor, which is the top floor—the penthouse. My father likes to be on top of everything that he does."

She eyed him with a speculative frown. "What is between you two? I know you didn't want to work for him and that you blame him for some of the problems in your parents' relationship, especially his inability to take your mom where she really wanted to go, but there's more, right?"

"A lot more, years of bad conversations and misunderstandings." He shrugged, not sure what else to say. He couldn't explain a lifetime with his father in a few minutes.

"And what?" she pressed.

"Have you ever had anyone in your life who made it their goal to take you down, to try to make you feel like a lesser person?"

"Carter did that, and I let him do it for too long, almost a year. I didn't realize it at the time. He claimed he was giving me helpful tips and constructive criticism. But I finally figured out that he just didn't like it when I came off better than him. Is that the problem with your dad?"

"Yes. He's been putting me down my entire life. Whatever I do is not good enough. As his son, I'm a reflection of him, and he wants to make me into what he considers to be his perfect mirror image. But I'm not him. I don't want to be him. And at this point in my life, I don't really care if we ever have a relationship."

"You must care somewhat or we wouldn't be going to this party."

She had a point. "It's more that I'm just tired of fighting."

She gave him a doubtful look. "That doesn't sound like you, Nick. You'll fight forever for what you want."

"Well, then maybe I just want to call a truce. I don't want to hate him. I don't want to work against him. I just want there to be nothing between us, not even anger."

"So you are trying to make some sort of peace with this appearance. I think that's good. Anger eats away at your soul. It's not good for you."

"I agree. It's just not that easy to get rid of, especially when the anger goes back a long time."

"Maybe getting the property your mom wanted, fulfilling her dream, will make it easier to let go of the resentment you have towards him."

"It feels like it should help, but I don't know." He pulled into a parking space designated for visitors and shut off the car. "It's not just that he didn't take her on the trip, Isabella. That disappointment for her just symbolizes all the other times he let her down and let me down. It's not like I can't understand that that particular trip didn't work out for many different reasons."

"It was just the last straw."

"Yes," he said, meeting her sympathetic gaze. "If you

want to know the real reason I'm going to this party, I'll tell you."

"Well, good, finally!"

"My father is my Achilles heel. Having any sort of emotion towards him or about that relationship weakens me. I don't like having any point of vulnerability. I need to cut the ties of anger, resentment, dislike and think of him as a stranger who means nothing to me."

"That's not going to work, Nick."

"I think it will."

"You're always going to have an emotional tie to your father. I have a tie to my dad, and I haven't seen him since I was thirteen years old. He didn't try to make me over or make me feel less of a person; he didn't care enough to even think about me."

"I'd prefer it if my father were absent from my life."

"That's easier to say when it's not true. But it's not just the part in your statement about your father that bothers me; it's that you consider caring about someone to be a weakness. You can't go through life like a robot. Business isn't everything. You could be the richest man in the world. You could have a thousand hotels, but it wouldn't change the fact that you need to love well as much as you need to live well."

Her passionate words made him want to love her, but love was weakening. It was painful and sometimes crippling, and he'd seen too many people falter in their careers and in their lives because they cared too much about what the wrong person thought.

Maybe if it were the right person...maybe then love would make a difference.

"Let's go to the party," he said abruptly. He got out of the car and waited for her to do the same.

She slammed the door as she exited. "I didn't think our conversation was over," she said with annoyance.

"For now it is."

"Just for the record, Nick, I don't like it when people tell me I'm done talking. Carter used to cut me off all the time. When he decided he'd had enough of a subject, we were done. That doesn't work for me."

He nodded, seeing the seriousness in her eyes. "Got it. And just for the record, Isabella, I heard everything you had to say. I just need to think about it."

His words dimmed the anger in her eyes.

"Okay, good."

He smiled. "Are we good, because there are going to be enough people at this party who don't like me. I'd prefer that the woman I'm with doesn't feel the same."

She sighed and gave him a frustrated smile. "I wish I didn't like you. That would make it easier."

He knew exactly what she meant.

Nick's father was tall; he hadn't lied about that. Isabella looked at the dark-haired, blue-eyed man who stood out in the crowded living room, not just because of his height, but also because of his manner, his charisma. Maybe the attention was centered on him because it was his birthday, but it was more likely it was because of the kind of man he was.

"That's him. That's Thomas Hunter," Nick said.

"I figured. You have similar features." She saw the tense lines around his eyes and mouth, and she impulsively took his hand in hers.

For a moment, he looked startled. She thought he might pull away, and then his fingers closed around hers.

"I've got your back," she said softly.

His gaze darkened. "I don't think anyone has ever said that to me before."

In that moment, she realized another truth about Nick. He'd grown up lonely, without a strong team behind him. No wonder he'd had to build such a strong wall around his heart and his emotions. He saw caring as a weakness because he'd felt weak as a child, wanting his parents' attention and love. But his mom and dad had apparently been too caught up in their own battles to see that their child needed more than he was getting.

She was very lucky that her mother had put her first even though it had made her life a lot more difficult. And while she hadn't been as close to her mother because of her many jobs, she'd always known that her mother was working to make her life better. She suspected that Nick felt his father had only worked to make his own life better.

"Nick."

The loud, booming voice of Thomas Hunter made Nick stand even straighter, and Isabella felt herself doing the same thing as if she, too, needed to square her shoulders and lift her chin and prepare for battle. This wasn't her fight, but she'd just declared herself as Nick's backup, so she needed to be ready.

"Dad," Nick said shortly. "Happy Birthday."

"Thanks for coming," Thomas said.

An awkward moment followed his words. The two men had made no move to physically connect with each other—no handshake, no hug, no slap on the back. The two feet of air between them couldn't be breached.

"Nicholas, how lovely that you could come." The woman standing next to Thomas didn't have the same reservations about touching. She came forward and extended her arms to Nick.

He let go of Isabella's hand to accept the woman's embrace, but he didn't really soften or smile. He was just being polite, she thought.

"Erica," he said. "You look beautiful as always."

"You're so sweet to say so."

Erica was a beautiful blonde with a stunningly pretty face. She was probably mid to late thirties. And it would have made more sense to see her with Nick than with his father, but obviously having a young, pretty girlfriend was part of Thomas Hunter's persona.

Erica stepped back and put her arm around Thomas's waist. "Your father and I were hoping you would come."

"Well, I'm here. This is Isabella Martinez—my father, Thomas Hunter, and his girlfriend, Erica Fox."

"It's nice to meet both of you, and Happy Birthday, Mr. Hunter," she added with a smile.

"Thank you," Thomas said. "Let's get you two some drinks." He motioned for a waiter. "Daniel will take care of you. Anything you want."

Isabella had a feeling that what Nick wanted was to be gone, but he did manage to order a gin and tonic from the waiter while she asked for a glass of wine.

"I have some people coming later that I want you to meet," Thomas said as the waiter left and Erica drifted away to speak to other friends. "David Adams from the Danforth Hedge Fund has an opportunity he wants to speak to you about. I think you should seriously consider it."

"I'm aware of his opportunity. I already told him I wasn't interested."

Thomas frowned. "How could you not be interested? The possibility of tremendous financial return is right in front of your face."

"It would require a larger investment than I'm willing to make right now. That money is earmarked for other ventures."

"You're not still talking about Argentina?"

"Plans are moving forward," Nick said evenly.

Isabella could see the strain in Thomas's eyes at that piece of news.

"It was a picture in a magazine that she liked, that's all it was, Nick. She never meant for you to build your whole life around it. I thought you would have figured that out by now. There's no room for sentiment in business."

"I'm going to buy the land in Argentina next week."

Thomas blew out an angry breath. "Well, fine, do it already. Then maybe you can move on."

"Like you have with Erica?" Nick bit out.

Isabella tensed, feeling the air grow thicker between them. They hadn't raised their voices, but their conversation was drawing the attention of some of the other guests, something she was sure that Nicholas would not want. It was time for backup.

"I'd love to see more of your beautiful home, Mr. Hunter," she interrupted. "Would it be possible to get a tour?"

He stared at her like she'd just asked him to show her the moon. Even Nick seemed bewildered by her sudden entrance into the conversation. She wasn't surprised. Their discussion hadn't really been about the land in Argentina but a lifetime of dissenting opinions and the inability to connect with each other.

"Of course," Thomas said finally. "I'd be happy to show you around.

"Great." She was thrilled that the waiter arrived at just that moment with her wine glass. "We'll be back," she told Nicholas.

"Take your time," he said shortly, draining his gin and tonic in one long swallow.

———◆◆◆———

"There are three bedrooms and a den. This is the master

suite," Thomas said as he led her into the massive and luxurious bedroom. One thing both father and son shared was a love for the finer things in life. "Erica did the decorating. That's how we met. She's an interior designer."

"She did an amazing job. I love the colors. So many people just use white. Or they pick off-white and think they're being adventurous."

He smiled, starting to relax. "Where did you meet my son, Isabella?"

"At my dance studio. I'm giving him tango lessons."

Thomas couldn't have looked more shocked. "Seriously?"

She nodded, not going into the reasons behind Nick's decision to learn the tango. "He'll be very good once he manages to loosen up and not worry about being perfect."

Thomas stared back at her. "He's talked to you about me, hasn't he?"

"A very little bit," she said honestly. "But I can see there's tension."

"That's putting it mildly." Thomas paused. "Is he unhappy that I'm with Erica?"

"He never mentioned her to me."

"I know she's a lot younger than I am, and most people think she's some sort of a trophy, but the truth is she just makes me feel like there's more to life. I like her positive attitude. She has so much self-confidence. I never have to worry about having to constantly pump her up, make her feel worthy. That can be exhausting."

She had the feeling he was talking about Nick's mother now.

"Are you and Nick serious about each other?" he asked, abruptly changing the subject.

"Oh, no. We're just—friends."

"Too bad. You seem like a smart woman."

"How would you know that?"

"You separated us before we could make a scene or throw a punch at the other." He gave her a dry smile. "We've never gotten along. I try to help Nick, but he wants nothing to do with me."

"Maybe you should stop trying to help him and just be his father."

"What kind of father doesn't try to help his kid?"

"I don't know. I'm not the expert on fathers. My dad wasn't even around when I was growing up. But I will say this. I think the fact that Nick is here shows there's hope for a better relationship—if you both decide you want to try for that."

"I hate to see him make mistakes because he's trying to make something up to his mother. She wouldn't have wanted him to do what he's done."

"Be successful?" Isabella challenged. "She wouldn't have wanted that?"

"She wouldn't have wanted him to chase a foolish dream she had one day sixteen years ago."

"I don't know if the dream was foolish or if Nick is still chasing it, but from what I can see of his business, it's not just about his mother's dream vacation spot. He's built a successful chain of hotels. He's young to have accomplished all that he has. And if you want my opinion—"

"I have a feeling you're going to give it to me even if I don't want it."

"I do have a tendency to butt in," she admitted.

"What's your opinion?"

"Nick takes after you, not his mom. He may have taken a different path, but if you really look, I think you'll see that your son is more like you than even he wants to be."

Thomas grinned. "I know he sure as hell doesn't *want* to be like me. I like you, Isabella. I hope you stick around, and

I'm not just talking about the party."

She was saved from answering by Erica's appearance in the bedroom. The younger woman gave them both a somewhat suspicious look.

"I thought you two got lost," she said, putting a possessive arm around Thomas. "Nick is looking for you, Isabella."

"Thanks for showing me around, Mr. Hunter."

"Please call me Thomas."

"I will. I'd better find Nick."

She was on her way back to the party in the living room when she saw Nick standing by the window in the den. He was gazing out at the view, and there was something about his hard profile that made her heart turn over. She knew now that the hardness was a cover for a kind, loving and loyal heart. But Nick rarely let down that cover.

"What are you doing in here?" she asked.

He jolted at her words, then turned his head. "Taking a break. I didn't think the apartment was that big. You've been gone a long time."

"I was talking to your dad."

"About what?"

"You."

He frowned. "You could have at least tried to pretend I wasn't the topic."

"Since you're pretty much the only thing your dad and I have in common, I didn't think you'd believe me." She paused for a moment. "He loves you, Nick."

Nick immediately shook his head. "He loves his idea of me, not who I really am."

"I don't think you show him who you really are."

"I used to. It didn't go well. It doesn't matter. I'm not going to change his mind about me, and he's not going to change my mind about him. Coming here was a mistake."

"No, it wasn't. You have to keep trying."

Nick gave her a sharp, warning look. "Isabella, you can't fix us, no matter how hard you try. Our relationship broke decades ago."

"Your mom was a bridge between you two, and when she died, you lost your bridge. But maybe someone else could help connect you."

"Someone like you?"

"Or Erica, or one of your other friends. I'm just saying I think you could have a relationship if you could find your way out of the past, forgive each other for some of the disappointments."

"I don't need a relationship with my father."

"Don't you? I wouldn't say anything if I thought you were happy with the way things are between you, but you're not. And we're here in your father's house. So why not talk to him?"

"I already spoke with him. He's trying to get me to make an investment I don't want to make."

"So don't talk business."

"We have nothing else in common."

She wondered if that were really true.

"I don't want to talk about him anymore."

"Then let's mingle."

His expression filled with distaste, and she couldn't help but laugh. "It is a party, Nick. That's what you do. There must be someone here you'd like to talk to."

"I'm talking to her," he said, gazing into her eyes. "Let's get out of here."

"After we get some food, I'm hungry."

"I'll buy you dinner anywhere you want."

"There's a beautiful buffet in the next room. We're here, Nick. Let's give it thirty minutes before we bail."

"I thought you had my back."

"I do. I'll be right behind you. Trust me, Nick. It's going to be fine. You might even have fun."

Fourteen

An hour later, Nick was actually glad that Isabella had encouraged him to stay at the party. Two cousins, twins Kari and Mick that he hadn't seen in at least eight or nine years, showed up, and it was fun to catch up with them. Their mother was his father's younger sister, Deirdre, and she'd always been a lot more fun than his dad. But Deirdre had moved to Arizona years ago, and her kids had gone with her. Apparently both had decided to come back and live in San Francisco.

Kari was working as a flight attendant and Mick as an architect. They were both funny and outgoing and reminded him of a time in his life, long before his mom had gotten sick, and his parents' marriage had gone sour, when he and his cousins had just enjoyed each other's company on family vacations and holidays.

Isabella fit right in with the group, too. She was the kind of person who could always find a friend. She was warm and interested in whatever anyone was saying, and most importantly, her interest was genuine. She liked getting to know new people, and he couldn't remember the last time he'd thought about trying to make a new friend. Not that he had time for friends. Business partners and coworkers fit his crazy lifestyle, but those relationships never went beneath the surface. He'd thought that's what he liked about those relationships, but now he felt like he'd been missing something.

It was Isabella who was making him rethink his life, he thought with a frown. He'd hired her to give him tango lessons, but now she was getting entangled in every other part of his life. It was probably good they wouldn't see each other after Argentina.

But even in his head that thought didn't sound good at all. He wanted to keep seeing her, but could he fit her into his life?

Could he fit into hers?

Of course they could both do what they needed to do—if they wanted to.

He was beginning to realize just how much he wanted to keep her in his life.

"This cake is amazing," Isabella said, giving him a big smile. She held up the dessert plate in her hand. "Do you want a bite?"

"No, I'm good."

"Okay, more for me." She finished the cake in two more bites and put the plate down on a nearby table. "Are you ready to leave?"

"I am."

"You lasted longer than I thought you would."

"It was fun to see Mick and Kari again."

"Yes, I didn't realize you had cousins. I thought your family was just your dad and you."

"My dad has three siblings, and I have ten cousins, but we're all spread out now, so we rarely see each other."

"It was good you came tonight. Shall we say goodbye to your dad?"

Nick saw his father in the middle of a conversation with two of his friends and decided to give that a pass. While they hadn't spoken since he'd first arrived at the party, he knew that his father was aware that he'd stayed, and that was good enough. "Let's just slip out. Mick and Kari already left. There's no one else I need to say goodbye to."

They made their way down to the parking garage in silence, not speaking until they were back in the car.

"Shall I take you home?" he asked halfheartedly, not really wanting the night to be over.

"I was thinking maybe we should stop by the hotel and run the tango a few times before you take me home. It's not far from here."

That was the last thing he wanted to do, but how could he say no? They were leaving for Argentina in two days, and he still didn't know the dance. "All right. I guess we should do that."

A knowing smile flitted across her mouth. "I love your enthusiasm."

"I don't like to do things I'm not good at."

"That's how you get better. You keep doing the things you're not good at and then you get good."

"There's also such a thing as talent."

"Talent only makes up a very small percentage of a successful person. Desire, determination and perseverance are usually what separates the 'almost there' person from the one who makes it all the way to the top."

"I believe that, too," he admitted. "But I'm not trying to get to the top of the dance world; I'm just hoping not to step on your feet or look like a fool."

"You won't step on my feet or look like a fool. I won't let that happen."

"I'm very glad you're coming with me."

With Isabella as his partner, all eyes would naturally be drawn to her. As long as he didn't screw up completely, he should be able to dance well enough to get Juan Carlos to sign on the dotted line.

"I'm excited about the trip and a little scared."

"You're worried because of your father?"

She nodded. "I spoke to my mother last night. She filled me in on more details of their marriage, including the fact that my dad apparently went to jail when I was in high school for embezzling funds from his employer to fund his substance abuse problems."

"I'm sorry. Did you have any idea?"

"About his going to jail—that was a shock. The substance abuse problems I kind of figured were part of why my parents split up. I overheard some conversations between my mother and my aunt over the years that led me to believe he was a big drinker."

"How does your mother feel about you going to Argentina?"

"She hates the idea, but she understands that it's my decision to make. I still haven't decided if I will try to speak to my father. My mom did give me my aunt's phone number. I can use it or not."

"Would you really be able to go all the way to Argentina and not look him up?" Nick asked doubtfully. "Aren't you the woman who just lectured me about the importance of family?"

"I don't think it was a lecture."

"You know what I mean."

"Your father has always been in your life, Nick. As much as you hate his interference, he's there interfering. My father abandoned me. I haven't seen him since I was thirteen. He wouldn't recognize me if we passed on the street. It's different for me than for you. I don't know what condition my father is in, or if he has any interest in reconnecting. He certainly hasn't made any effort on his end. And maybe he doesn't deserve to see me, to know how I've grown up, what I've done with my life. Why should I put myself out there when he's never shown any interest in me?"

You're making a good argument for not looking him up. It might be better to leave it alone. You have to look at the ROI."

"The what?" she asked in confusion.

"Return on investment. You'd be investing your heart in this reunion. You have a lot to lose if it doesn't go well. Your father doesn't have anything to lose. He was an adult when he walked away from you. He made a conscious choice. You were a child. You didn't have a choice then, but you have one now."

"It might be the hardest decision I've ever had to make."

"Speaking of decisions…any other thoughts on taking the stage again?"

She gave a little sigh. "I told the Tylers I'd tell them on Monday. I'm giving myself a few days to think about it."

He pulled up in front of the hotel. As he got out of the car, he handed his keys to the valet and said, "I'll be about an hour."

"It must be nice to have so many people do your bidding," Isabella said lightly as they walked into the hotel.

"Actually, we offer valet parking to anyone who wants it," he returned.

"You know that's not what I meant. You live a big life. Mine is small in comparison."

"It's only small if you want it to be. If you don't, change it."

"You make it sound easy."

"It's definitely *not* easy. Nothing that's good is ever easy."

She laughed.

"What did I say?" he asked warily.

"You should remember what you just said when we start dancing."

"I set myself up for that, didn't I?"

"You did."

He opened the door for her. "After you."

She didn't know what had changed between the last tango lesson and this one, but Nick was the most relaxed she'd ever seen him.

"Did you have a lot to drink tonight?" she asked as they finished running through the first set of steps.

He laughed at the question. "I wouldn't have driven if I had drunk too much, so no."

"You're not as tense as you have been in the past."

"I'm starting to feel more confident. Let's try it with the music this time."

"All right." She turned on the music, then came back to him.

He pulled her into their starting position with the confidence he'd just mentioned, his hands holding hers with a firmness that told her he was ready to lead. They waited through a couple of beats, and then Max took the first step.

It was clear within minutes that he hadn't just improved a little but a lot. There were a few stumbles, and he swore under his breath after one screwed-up combination, but he didn't quit. He recovered and he kept going and when the music ended, she was breathless and happy.

"That's the first time we've made it all the way to the end," she said, impulsively putting her arms around him to give him a hug.

Nick returned the hug. When it should have ended, he held on. His blue eyes met hers. The emotions of the night, of the dance, swirled in each heated breath. The triumph in his gaze turned to desire. His lips tightened. His head slowly lowered.

The first touch of his lips against hers was a small spark that lit the explosiveness of the next kiss. He pulled her body up hard against his, his tongue sliding into her mouth, his hard chest against her soft breasts, his legs moving between hers, until she could feel every glorious male inch of him.

She moved her hands up and down his back, feeling the play of muscles under his shirt. It wasn't enough, so she pulled frantically on the material until it came free of his belted slacks. His skin was hot to her impatient fingers. She felt like he was burning up, and so was she. There was a fever between them that had been brewing for weeks.

This was no small attraction. This was a deep-rooted need that came from her heart, maybe her soul, and it was exhilarating and terrifying.

She needed to stop kissing him, stop touching him, stop wanting him...

But she couldn't find the strength. One more kiss, one more touch, one more minute.

A door burst open. Someone exclaimed something in Spanish.

She lifted her head in a daze, Nick doing the same.

She saw a crew of workers scurrying back out the door.

"Cleaning crew," Nick muttered, gazing back down at her. "We should take this somewhere else."

"Or maybe not." She licked her lips. "I don't think we should do this now." She stepped out of his embrace. It was a lot easier to think when he wasn't touching her. "It's late. I should go home. I have classes all day tomorrow, and we have to go to Argentina in a few days."

"Yeah," he said, a grim note to his voice. "All right. I'll take you back to your apartment, if you're sure that's what you want."

She couldn't pretend that she hadn't heard the challenge

in his voice. She licked her lips, feeling nervous and tense and not at all sure of what she wanted to happen next. Taking things further with Nick would no doubt be amazing. Maybe a few years ago, she wouldn't have thought that much about it. But she'd gotten more cautious since Carter, unwilling to invest more than the other person was investing, and with Nick she had no idea if he was willing to invest anything more than a few hours of fun.

"I think it's the best decision for now," she said.

"I thought you were the woman who lived in the moment, and I was the one who thought too much."

"Maybe you're rubbing off on me," she said lightly.

"Maybe you're rubbing off on me," he grumbled. "Because every time you kiss me, I stop thinking completely."

"I think you kissed me," she countered.

He smiled. "You want to argue about it?"

Arguing and fighting seemed the less dangerous choice. "Just pointing out the facts. Anyway..." She walked over to the stereo system and unplugged her player. When she glanced back at Nick, he was tucking his shirt back into his pants, reminding her of just how much she'd liked touching him and how much she wanted to see him without that shirt and without those pants. Another breath of frustration escaped her lips.

Nick met her gaze and amusement flashed through his eyes. He knew exactly what she was thinking. Damn him.

"So," she said, needing to change the subject. I think you're ready for Argentina, Nick."

"Tonight was a lot better, but I wouldn't say I'm ready. I still made a lot of mistakes."

"Not as many as last time, and you did better once you stopped worrying about being perfect and just danced. If you do that again for your business associate, he'll be satisfied."

"Satisfied, huh? That will make one of us."

And just like that they were back to the potent and inconvenient chemistry between them.

"What am I going to do about you, Isabella?"

"In a few days you'll say goodbye," she told him.

"Is that what you want to happen?"

"I don't know," she said honestly. She couldn't really imagine not seeing Nick again, not talking to him, or spending time with him, or kissing him again. "We live in different worlds. We both have a lot going on. I have some big decisions to make about my career, the studio, the direction I want my future to take. Those decisions all have the potential to change my life in a huge way. Part of me just wants to say no to everything because what I know, what I have, is good enough."

"And the other part of you?"

"Wants more. I want to risk it all, to be the woman I used to be—completely fearless."

"That's the woman you should be, Isabella. Your aunt told me you were born to fly, and that buying the studio would be like tying a ball and chain around your legs. That's why I made sure you got to that audition. I want to help you, but I don't want to be your ball and chain."

"Even if I were asking you to be?"

"Even then. You've forced me to look at my life differently the past few days. Maybe you should do the same."

"How are you looking at your life now?" she asked, wondering what he meant by his words.

"Like something that isn't as complete as I thought it was."

"So you want more, too."

"I always want more. Wanting more isn't my problem. Wanting the right things is a different story."

"So what happens next? What happens after you get your resort in Argentina?"

"I haven't thought beyond Argentina. It's been my driving goal for a decade."

"A goal you're going to reach in a few days," she reminded him.

"If I successfully dance the tango."

"You will. I won't let you fail. It's time to start thinking about what's next."

"You're right. Looks like we both have some decisions to make." He paused. "I'll take you home now, and in case you're wondering or worrying, I won't ask to come up, and you won't invite me in."

"I won't?" She couldn't help questioning his authoritative tone.

"No." He put his finger under her chin and tipped her gaze up to meet his. "The next time we kiss, we're not going to stop, Isabella. I think we both know that."

His words sent a shiver down her spine. She was tempted to kiss him right now and see what would happen...but the risk-taking part of her personality was still not quite ready to come out.

Fifteen

Isabella didn't see Nick on Thursday. Her day was filled with back-to-back classes and discussions with contractors. The studio repairs were on hold until Monday when Isabella would be forced to make a decision to either buy her aunt out or let the studio go to Karen Halley. The more she learned about the costs of running the studio, the more she realized that if she chose to take over the studio, her life would be more about management and business than about dancing.

She could hire a manager to take care of some of it, but it would still take up a lot of her time. She needed to factor that in to her decision.

She'd also received a script from the Tylers with a box of Godiva chocolates, her favorite, and a personal note from Donna expressing how much they wanted her to be part of the show. They planned on rewriting the featured role to emphasize her particular talents if she agreed to take it on.

She'd never had a producer go to so much trouble to get her in a show, and she couldn't deny that she was more than a little flattered and very, very tempted.

But at the moment, all those decisions were on hold until after Argentina.

On Friday afternoon, a limo picked her up a little after three o'clock in the afternoon and drove her to San Francisco International Airport. Nick was waiting for her in his luxurious private plane.

Her jaw dropped when she entered the plane. She'd never even flown first-class before, so a private plane was beyond her wildest dreams. The plush leather seats and tables made her feel like she was walking into someone's living room.

Nick was sitting at a table for four talking to Martin. They both had their computers open, and it was clear they were working. But as soon as Nick saw her, he stopped in mid-sentence and jumped to his feet, a smile spreading across his lips and a welcoming sparkle appearing in his eyes.

"Isabella," he said. "You made it."

"I'm here," She set down her tote bag on the nearest chair. "This is a gorgeous plane."

"Always the best for Nick," Martin cut in. "Nice to see you again, Isabella."

"You, too. I didn't realize you were coming as well." She was actually happy to see Martin, who would be a good chaperone for the fourteen-hour flight.

"Can I get you something to drink?" a steward asked her.

"I'm fine for now." She turned back to Nick. "Is anyone else coming?"

"No, it will just be the three of us," Nick replied. "Sit wherever you like. The seats at the back of the plane turn into beds, so hopefully you'll be able to sleep at some point."

"I'm too excited to think of sleeping. It's going to be so strange going back to the country where I was born. It feels like a million years since I was there."

"Why don't you sit at the table with us until we take off."

She took the chair he was offering. "I don't want to interrupt your work."

"It will wait," Nick said.

"So is Nick going to be able to dance without falling on his face?" Martin asked.

"Absolutely," she said. "I'm confident he will wow the

audience."

"Wow, huh?" Martin echoed. "That's more than I'm expecting."

"And Isabella is being overly optimistic," Nick said dryly. "I'm just hoping for passable."

"Nick tells me you were born in Argentina and still have some family there," Martin said.

"Yes, but I haven't seen anyone from that side of the family in a very long time. I'm not sure I'll see them now. I have my aunt's phone number. She lives in Buenos Aires so I might be able to see her."

"If you want to see her, we'll make that happen," Nick said.

"Thanks," she said. "I haven't decided yet."

"You're running out of time."

"I have at least fourteen hours."

"True."

The steward asked them to fasten their seatbelts. They'd been cleared for take-off.

Isabella fastened her belt with somewhat shaky fingers. She wasn't scared to fly, but she did feel like she was taking off on an adventure that would change her life.

Several minutes later, the small plane took off with speed and grace and they were soaring over the city of San Francisco. A long right turn sent them south—back to the country where her life had begun.

As they flew through the late afternoon, Nick and Martin worked on their computers while she watched a video.

Later, during dinner, they talked and laughed—a lot. Watch Nick and Martin interact gave Isabella an opportunity to see Nick's more lighthearted side. While it was clear that Nick was the boss, Martin was obviously like a brother to him. Martin was more than happy to share any story that made Nick look less than perfect. Nick also told some tales on Martin. The two men had shared many experiences over the last ten years.

"You two must have broken a lot of hearts," she murmured, thinking how the dark-haired Nick and the fair-haired Martin would stand out in any crowd. But add in wealth and power, and they'd no doubt been the target of many a single woman. "How are you both still single?"

"Martin isn't that single," Nick interjected. "He's been seeing a beautiful, generous, funny woman for almost three years. He just needs to put a ring on her finger."

"What I need is to stay in town long enough to plan a decent proposal," Martin said. "Maybe after we get the Argentina project off the ground, I'll be able to do that."

"What kind of proposal do you want to make?" she asked curiously.

"Something romantic. Got any good ideas?"

"Not really. I'm not big on grand gestures. I'd rather have something intimate and personal. You love me. I love you. Let's be together forever. That's all a woman really wants to hear."

"As long as the words come with a big diamond, right?" Martin asked.

She laughed. "That helps, I suppose."

As they moved on to dessert, their conversation turned to other topics.

Over the next few hours she learned a lot more about Nick—his favorite sports teams, his longest bike ride, the last movie he'd seen, the book he was currently reading. While so much of his focus was on business, especially when it came to the nonfiction books on his e-reader, he did seem to take some time to have a life. Hopefully, in the future he would take even more time. He'd worked very hard to get this life he was leading; now he had to learn how to enjoy it and maybe find someone to enjoy it with.

The idea that that *someone* might be her was enough to send a tingle down her spine and make her heart beat a little faster. Thank goodness Martin was on the plane, or she might be tempted to start the kiss that would never end...

—▸▶◀◂—

Nick hadn't slept more than an hour on the flight, mostly because he'd been distracted by watching Isabella sleep and fighting all kinds of restless urges to join her at the back of the plane.

What the hell had he been thinking having Martin go along on the trip? He and Isabella could have spent a really spectacular fourteen hours together. But then what?

Until he knew the answer to that question, he needed to keep his hands off of her. The last thing he wanted to do was hurt her like she'd been hurt before. He also didn't want to put his own heart on the line until...

Until what?

Wasn't his heart already on the line?

He hadn't stopped thinking about her for more than five minutes since they'd first met. She'd gotten into his head, his heart and way under his skin. She'd changed the way he thought about his career, his family, and his life. She'd reminded him that there were things he'd given up in his drive to get to the top, to be the best.

He didn't have regrets, because he didn't believe in regrets. But Isabella had made him think about what he wanted for his future, a future that would be wide open after he bought the Argentina property. He really hadn't given much thought to what would be next. It had taken him so long to get here, and he was so close to victory, he could taste it.

Which was why he couldn't let himself be distracted now.

Deliberatcly, he forced his gaze away from the sleeping Isabella and sat down at the table. An hour later, both Isabella and Martin were up and eating breakfast with him. An hour after that, the plane began its descent into the Buenos Aires International Airport. It was just after cleven o'clock on Saturday morning when he caught his first real glimpse of land. But he found himself looking away from the coastline where his dreams were about to come true to gaze at Isabella. Her cheeks were flushed pink, her brown eyes filled with excitement.

"Does it look like home?" he asked, following her gaze out the window.

"I'm not sure. I was eight years old when I left. I have a few memories of my life here, a couple of photos that my mother didn't throw away, but not many."

"The memories will come back. "What do you want to do when we land? I was going to suggest getting settled into the hotel, maybe taking a nap, but you look way too energized for that."

I couldn't possibly sleep. I'd like to walk around a bit if we have time."

"We do. Today is completely free. We'll stay in a hotel in the city tonight, and tomorrow morning we'll drive out to the property, talk to Juan Carlos and dance for him and his friends in the evening. We'll spend the night at his home, then return to Buenos Aires on Monday and fly home."

She nodded. "All right. That sounds fine. I'm happy to have today to explore a bit."

"I'll go with you."

"You don't have to do any work?"

"Martin can handle the business we have in Buenos Aires on his own."

Martin gave him a somewhat disbelieving smile, which Nick completely understood. It was extremely rare that he let

Martin take over business when they were traveling. But he didn't want to leave Isabella on her own. She'd come to Argentina for him, and he had a feeling it was going to be an emotional trip for her. She'd backed him up at his father's party. He'd return the favor now.

"That's right, I'll do all the work," Martin grumbled. "You two have a good time."

"We will," Nick said, fastening his seatbelt as the plane came in for landing.

—➤➤◀◀—

Buenos Aires was sunny, warm and welcoming, Isabella thought as she and Nicholas walked out of the hotel on Saturday afternoon. She'd taken only a few moments to unpack her small suitcase, take a shower, and change into a coral-colored knit top, ankle-length white jeans and a pair of flat sandals.

Nick had also changed from the flight, putting on slim dark jeans and a short-sleeved shirt. He looked more like a man on vacation than a man on a mission. She was happy to see him relaxed and in the mood to explore the city with her.

"The hotel has offered us a driver for the day," he told her.

"Oh, no, I'd rather walk. We'll be able to see more."

"I had a feeling you would say that. Let's go." He slid on a pair of sunglasses and took her hand in his. "So I don't get lost," he said with a smile.

"You're in a good mood."

"I am," he agreed. "How about you?"

"Same. Eager to see the city again."

"Is this area familiar to you?"

"It is."

Their hotel was located on Calle Florida, a wide street

filled with hotels, restaurants and boutiques in the more upscale section of the city. While things had definitely changed in the last eighteen years, some of the buildings looked quite familiar, and as they walked past a park, she distinctly remembered a family picnic with her father's family.

"We had a birthday party here." She paused by a large fountain. "At those tables over there." She pointed across the park. "My cousin Liliana turned twelve. I must have been seven at the time. It wasn't long before we went to San Francisco."

"It's a nice spot for a party."

"Yes," she said, feeling a bit of sadness that she'd lost all touch with that side of her family. "Let's keep walking."

Nick didn't say much as they strolled through the streets, letting her absorb the sights and sounds of her homeland. Every now and then he related some fact, usually relating to architecture. It was clear he'd done his research on the city, but while she appreciated some of his insight, she was so caught up in emotions she could barely register what he was saying. Every step, every block, brought her closer to a decision she needed to make.

When they finally returned to the hotel several hours later, she was tired but resolved.

"I need to call my aunt," she said, stopping abruptly as they entered the lobby.

"Okay. Do you want to call from your room?"

"I think I should do it now." She pulled out her cell phone. "And maybe you could stay."

"Whatever you want, Isabella. Let's go over there. It's quieter."

She followed him to an empty seating area in the far corner of the lobby. They sat down on the couch together.

"I'm nervous," she said. "I don't know what to expect."

"How could you know? It's been a long time. But whatever happens, Isabella, you're going to be okay. You know that, right? You're an amazing woman. And you're you. Wherever you came from, whoever your parents are, whatever choices they made doesn't change who you are."

She nodded as his confident words made her sit up a little straighter. She punched in her aunt's phone number and waited for the first ring. Her heart was racing a thousand miles a minute, and when a man's voice came across the line, she felt suddenly dizzy with fear and excitement. Was that her father's voice? The tone sounded so familiar.

"Papa?" she heard herself say.

"¿Quién llama"

"It's Isabella."

There was a silence at the other end of the phone. She heard a woman ask who was on the phone. The man said her name. And in that second she knew she had not been talking to her father, because there was no recognition in his voice.

"Isabella?" The woman's voice came over the line. "Is that really you?"

"Yes, it's me," she said, happy to be speaking in English to her Aunt Carlotta. She barely remembered Spanish. After they'd gone back to San Francisco, her mother had made a point to only speak in English. She hadn't even let Isabella take Spanish in school, insisting she learn French instead. "My mother gave me your number. I'm in Buenos Aires, and I'd like to speak to my father. Do you know where I can reach him?" Another long minute passed. "Please, I know it's been a long time, but I would like to talk to him."

"I'm sorry, Isabella," Carlotta said. "Your father is not here, and I don't know where he is."

"You must have some idea," she said, feeling a little desperate now that she'd come this far. She didn't want everything to end with a phone call.

"He's been away for a long time, Isabella. He hasn't been well. We've tried to help him, but he always disappears. I know that's not what you want to hear. I wish I could tell you that your father is a wonderful man and that he regrets leaving you and your mother. I wish I could say all those things, because I adored my brother for a very long time, too long, really. I made excuses for him. I blamed your mother for some of his problems. I didn't keep in touch with her or with you, and you were family—both of you. Instead, I chose to be on the side of a man who couldn't be there for anyone in his family."

Her hand tightened on the phone as Carlotta's words brought tears to her eyes. "You really don't know where he is?"

"Well, you might be able to find him at one of his favorite bars. I can give you a list, but I have to warn you that he's a broken man, Isabella. He's not just an alcoholic; he has a mental illness. I think you should remember Diego as he was and not as he is now. He would want that, too. He used to tell me in the occasional sober moment that the only good that had ever come out of his life was you and that he was happy that you were far, far away from him and couldn't see how badly he'd destroyed his life."

There was a part of Isabella that wanted to hang on to the memory and not see the reality, but there was another part of her that felt like she needed to look that man in the face and see what everyone else saw. "Tell me where I might be able to find him," she said.

Carlotta gave her the names of three bars and then said, "If you'd like to come by tonight, I would love to see you. I can invite Liliana over. She lives close by. She would love to see her little cousin."

Isabella hesitated, putting her hand over the phone as she turned to Nick. "Would it be all right if I saw my aunt tonight?"

"Of course. Can I come?"

"Do you want to?"

"I'll be your backup," he said.

She gave him an emotion-filled smile. "Thanks." She lifted her hand off the phone. "I would like to come by, and I'll have a friend with me."

"What time shall we expect you?"

"Seven or eight? I'm going to see if I can find my father first."

"If you do, tell him we miss him, and he can always come to my house."

"I will." She jotted down Carlotta's address and then ended the call. "Did you hear any of that?"

"I got the feeling your father is still dealing with alcohol issues."

"My aunt says he's sick, and they've done everything they can to try to help him. She doesn't think I should look for him, but she did give me the names of some of his favorite bars."

"What do you want to do?"

"I'd like to try to find him. I feel like I've come this far. I can't just fly home without giving it a shot. Maybe I could help him."

Nick frowned at that statement. "You can't fix him, Isabella."

"You don't know that. You don't know him."

"I know that if his family hasn't been able to help him, it's doubtful his long-lost daughter will be able to work a miracle."

"But I am his daughter, and I wouldn't be the amazing woman you said I was if I didn't try."

"Well, that's true," he said with a smile. "Are we leaving now?"

"I feel like it's now or never."

"Okay, but I'm going to see if we can get a car and a driver for this excursion."

"Good idea. I have no idea how far any of these places are."

"Or what kind of neighborhood they're in," Nick said.

She met his gaze and realized that finding her father might take her into places she'd never wanted to go. But Nick would be with her, and knowing that gave her courage.

Isabella's determination to find her father faltered after the first dive bar and got weaker after the second. But Nick kept her going. She had one more chance, and she had to take it.

Last on the list was La Puerta Blanco, located on the outskirts of the city, far from the tourist action. Isabella was more than happy to have Nick by her side when they entered the dimly lit bar. The bar was fairly empty; it was barely seven on a Saturday night. The crowd probably wouldn't arrive until at least eleven. If there was a crowd, she silently amended, noting that most of the patrons seemed to be well past their forties and many seemed to be alone.

There was one man sitting at the bar who drew her gaze. He sat with hunched shoulders, as if he wished he could disappear into his own body. His hair was pepper gray, stringy and drifted past his collar. He yelled something in Spanish at the soccer match being played on the television behind the bar. Then he asked for another shot of tequila.

She wanted to turn around and leave but there was something about his voice that was very familiar to her.

She was suddenly terrified—was this man her father? Did she really want to know for sure?

Her mother had told her she would be disappointed if she made contact.

Her aunt had said that her father was a broken man and it would be best for her to remember him the way he was.

"I don't know what to do," she murmured.

Nick put his arm around her. "Yes, you do."

She looked up at him, and his gaze held hers for a long minute. She saw both admiration and concern in his eyes, but he wasn't expressing that concern. He was letting her make up her own mind.

"Okay." She drew in a breath to calm her nerves and then walked up to the man at the bar. "Diego Martinez?"

The man turned his head in confusion. "Sí?"

Her heart thumped against her chest as she stared into his dark eyes. His face was familiar and yet not. His gray bearded cheeks were hollow, and his skin was pale. He looked like the ghost of the man she'd once known.

"I'm Isabella," she said.

He blinked in confusion. Then he reached into his pocket and pulled out his wallet. A moment later he was handing her a faded photo. It was the picture they'd taken together at her eighth-grade graduation. Tears filled her eyes.

"This is me," she said. "I'm Isabella."

He shook his head as if he didn't understand her. "Is she well? Is she safe?"

She licked her lips as a tear slipped down her cheek. He didn't recognize her. He didn't understand that his daughter was standing right in front of him. Her aunt had told her there was more wrong with him than an addiction to alcohol, and she could see that clearly now.

"Bella—so beautiful," he murmured, a far-away expression in his eyes. "Smart like her mother. But she danced like me."

"She did?"

"On my feet. She would put her feet on mine, and I would spin her around the room. She loved that so much."

The memory of that long-forgotten moment hit her square in the chest, squeezing hard at her heart. "She did love that. She loved you, too. She wants you to get help."

He shook his head. "I'm beyond help. Ask anyone. Ask Roberto here. He knows."

Isabella glanced over at the middle-aged overweight bartender who gave her an uncaring shrug.

"Do you have somewhere to sleep tonight?" she asked her father. "Carlotta said you're welcome at her house."

Surprise filled through his eyes. "You know Carlotta?"

"She told me where to find you. She wants you to come home."

"No, she doesn't. She told me to get out and never come back. Couldn't blame her. I stole money from her."

"She's forgiven you."

"I need another shot." He lifted his empty glass and pounded it down on the bar.

The bartender ambled over, refilled the glass, and then moved back to help another customer.

Her father threw back the shot and let out a sigh of appreciation.

She decided to make one last attempt. "I'm Isabella. I'm your daughter."

He stared back at her, and this time his gaze just seemed empty. Then he said, "Tell Isabella I love her."

"Okay," she said, giving up.

Her father got up from the barstool and headed for the men's room.

She looked at Nick.

He stepped forward and wiped a tear from her cheek. "You all right?"

"He didn't know me. He didn't understand."

"Maybe he did—somewhere in his head. Do you want to wait for him to come out?"

She shook her head. "No, I'm done here."

They walked out of the bar and got back into the car. She held it together for about two minutes, and then the tears came followed by the choking sobs.

Nick put his arms around her and let her cry her way back to the city. She didn't know where he told the driver to go, but eventually they ended up at a small market. The driver went inside and came back with a box of tissues.

She wiped her eyes and blew her nose and tried to pull herself together. "Sorry about that. I got your shirt all wet." She gave him a watery smile.

He tucked a strand of her hair behind one ear. "It will dry. Feel any better?"

"I actually do feel better."

"Sometimes tears are good."

"You've probably never cried a day in your life."

"Not true. I cried when my mother died. Not where anyone could see me, but there were a few tears."

"Everyone cries when a parent dies. That's understandable. But my father is alive."

"Not in the way you want him to be. He's sick, and your tears were an expression of grief for the loss of the man you'd held in your heart all these years."

"You're right. I don't know why he couldn't understand that he was looking at me—at his daughter."

"But he told you to tell Isabella that he loved her. That's what you wanted to hear, isn't it?"

"I guess. But I wanted him to know he was talking to me."

"You know that he loved you and that he still does. That's what's important. That's what you have to take away from this."

"I wish I could help him get better."

"I'm sure everyone in his family feels that way. Some people can't be helped. I know you don't want to believe that, but it's true."

"I don't want to believe that. I should have stayed in the bar and tried to get through to him."

"You did try. He didn't want you to get through to him. You told him he could go to his sister's place, and he said he stole money from her."

"She didn't tell me that."

"Addiction is complicated and horrifically painful to watch anyone you love go through. I didn't have it in my family, but I had a friend in college who went to the dark side, and a lot of people have tried to help him and failed. It drives his family crazy to know that they can't fix him. I suspect your aunt has had a lot of years of pain because of your father's disease."

"I still want to see her," she said. "How horrible do I look right now?"

He smiled. "You look like you've been through a battle—but it was a battle you won."

"Did I?"

"What do you think?"

She thought for a long moment and came to the only conclusion that made sense. "I don't feel like I won anything, but I'm glad that I saw him. I'm sad that he's the way he is. I will talk to my aunt about him. Maybe there's something I can do to help her help him. I know you'll think I'm a fool for having any hope that he could be helped, but—"

"But that's who you are," he finished. "You're fiercely loyal to the people you love, and you'd do anything to help someone in trouble. Like I said before, you're an amazing woman, and tonight your father got to see that."

"He didn't know it was me."

"I think that somewhere in his head he knew it was you."

She didn't know if she could believe that, but it made her feel better to think it was true. "Thanks for going with me, Nick. Hopefully, having dinner with my aunt will not be so emotional or dramatic."

An hour later, she knew she was half right. There was no drama at her aunt's house, but there were plenty of emotions. Not only was her Aunt Carlotta there, but her cousin Liliana, and her boyfriend, and her other cousin Enrique and his wife and their twin babies. They greeted her with warm, loving hugs and a few tears, but these were happy tears. The family that had once been shattered was coming back together.

Her father was a big topic of conversation. She learned more about her dad's jail term and his many failed attempts at sobriety as well as a late diagnosis of mental illness. Her aunt confirmed that her father did speak of Isabella but never seemed to understand that his little girl might be grown up by now.

It was sad to know that there seemed to be little hope for her dad, but it was wonderful to reconnect with that side of the family.

Dinner was a lively affair with lots of conversation and many stories about the past. She worried that Nick might be a little bored, but he gave no indication of it, and he was fully engaged with everyone in the room. In fact, he seemed to enjoy hearing about her early years and how she'd been as a little kid. No one else in her life had ever heard about her childhood in Argentina, and the fact that Nick now knew so much about her made her feel even closer to him.

She was beginning to wonder how she was ever going to say goodbye to the man.

But she had a few more days before she had to do that, so she was going to enjoy the time they had together and let the future bring whatever it was supposed to bring.

Sixteen

Nick waited in the lobby on Sunday morning for Isabella to come down. After the disturbing talk with her father, the emotional reunion with her family, not to mention the jet lag, she was probably exhausted. He hoped she'd have enough energy to dance later, because today was the big day.

Martin stepped off the elevator and gave him a nod. "Are you ready to go?"

"As soon as Isabella comes downstairs."

"What did you and Isabella do yesterday while I was taking care of business?" Martin asked with a dry smile.

"We walked around the city. I saw a lot of Buenos Aires. Then last night we had dinner with some of her relatives."

Martin raised an eyebrow at that piece of information. "You hung out with Isabella's family? You—the man who rarely spends time with his own family?"

He shrugged. "It was fun."

"That's another word you don't use very often."

"I was mixing it up with the locals. That's what Juan Carlos wanted, right? Last time I mucked things up by spending all my time in the hotel studying the financials. I won't make that mistake again."

"Good, because if you'd done all that on the last trip, we

wouldn't be here now. We'd have a signed contract and would probably be breaking ground on the resort."

"Don't remind me," he said with a little sigh. "I'm very aware of how much time we've lost."

"So when you were mixing it up with the locals last night, were you also mixing it up with Isabella? Because she is one beautiful woman."

"Not in the way you're suggesting," he said quickly. "It's not like that—well, not exactly like that."

"You're into her, Nick. Admit it."

"I admit it," he said easily. "I like her, but it's complicated."

"Is it? Or are you just making it complicated? Isabella is attractive, warm, funny, smart…she's the whole package. What don't you like?"

"She's emotional. She thinks with her heart—when she thinks at all. Mostly, she just goes with her gut and leaps without looking. That's not who I am."

"Definitely not," Martin agreed. "But maybe that's all good. You don't want another version of yourself. You want a woman who challenges you. I think she does that."

"She also may be taking a job in the theater, dancing in some new musical. She could be traveling, on the road for weeks, maybe ending up in New York."

"Really? I thought you were trying to help her buy her studio."

"She has another option, one she should really take. I've seen her dance, and she could set Broadway on fire."

"So what happens next?" Martin asked.

"I don't know."

"You always know, Nick. Why not this time? What's different? And don't tell me you haven't given it any thought, because you always give everything a lot of thought."

"She's different—she's important. I don't want to screw it

up," he said honestly. "I don't want to start something I can't finish."

Martin looked at him in surprise. "I've never heard you sound so serious about a woman before. Maybe she's the one."

His pulse leapt when Martin said the words aloud that had been running through his mind the last few days. Fortunately, he was saved from a reply when Isabella joined them with an apologetic smile. While her eyes were tired, she also looked happy to be up and ready for another adventure. She'd left her hair down and wore a floral dress that clung to her curves; her beautiful legs were bare, her feet accented by a pair of high wedge sandals.

"Sorry, to keep you waiting," she said. "I slept through the alarm. I don't usually sleep this late."

"Jet lag and time zone changes," he said. "It's not a problem."

"Good. How are you, Martin?"

"Great. Eager to get to the show tonight," Martin said. "I can't wait to see you two—dance together."

Nick saw the wicked light in Martin's eyes and gave him a silent glare that told him to behave. Not that that would have much effect on Martin, who apparently felt enough job security to say whatever was on his mind.

"You're going to be impressed," Isabella told Martin as they walked out of the hotel and got into the waiting SUV. "Nick is going to knock your socks off with his smooth moves."

"That is something I can't wait to see," Martin said, giving Nick another sly look before taking the seat in the back of the vehicle. He immediately put on his headphones. "You two feel free to talk. I'm going to listen to Joel's webinar on international sales strategies."

There would have been a time when he might have

listened to that, too, or spent the ninety-minute drive to Juan Carlos's house talking on the phone or reviewing the plans for the project. But now he was more interested in talking to Isabella.

He sat down on the bench seat next to Isabella and fastened his seat belt. "Did you get any sleep last night?"

"It took me awhile to calm my brain down," she admitted. "I had a lot to think about, but I'm happy the night ended on a better note than it started."

"Your family was entertaining. Do you think you'll keep in touch?"

"Definitely. Liliana said she's planning a trip to California next summer, so I will see her then."

"How do you think your mother will feel about you reconnecting with your father's side of the family?"

"I'm not sure. But I think—I hope—she'll be open to it. Carlotta acknowledged that she hadn't treated my mother well and had blamed her for a lot of my father's problems. If she is willing to tell my mother that, it will definitely help pave the path to a truce." Isabella blew out a breath. "I can't thank you enough for going with me, Nick. I wouldn't have made it into those disgusting bars if you hadn't been with me. And I wouldn't have seen my father."

He wasn't sure it was such a great thing for her to have found her father in the condition the man was in, but if she was happy, he was happy. "No problem."

She looked out the window as they got onto the highway. "I'm excited to get out of the city. It will be fun to see more of the country."

"Did you take many trips out of the city when you were young?"

"I'm quite sure we went to some beaches, but I don't remember where they were."

"Well, you're about to be driven through some of the

most beautiful land in the world."

"You really do love this country, don't you?" she asked, giving him a thoughtful smile. "You're not faking it to get the deal. You love Argentina."

"I don't know about love, but I do like it here. And I believe the resort will do extremely well, both for me and for the local economy."

"Are you nervous about dancing tonight?"

Actually, he wasn't as stressed about that as he'd thought he would be. A lot had happened in the past week that had shifted his focus—in a good way. He hadn't thought he was living in a narrow world until that world had been blown wide open. Who would have thought a tango teacher from Argentina could have done that?

"Why are you smiling?" Isabella asked curiously.

He shrugged. "It's just a good day."

She nodded, meeting his gaze. "I think so, too."

He could have gone on looking at her forever, but eventually she turned toward the window. "I can't wait to see your beach, Nick."

"It looks like the picture I showed you. I wasn't sure it would, because rarely does anything look the same after so many years have passed, but it did. The hotel, however, didn't fare so well."

She gave him a quick look. "The hotel?"

"The small hotel where my mother wanted to stay. It had only eight rooms, but four of them had beautiful ocean views. And one of them was only a step away from the sand. The grandparents of the man I'm doing business with now—Juan Carlos—owned the hotel for forty years, but they've both passed away, and while Juan has plenty of money and will soon have a lot more, he's decided to let the hotel be torn down to make way for my resort. He told me that his grandmother had always wanted a bigger place, so rather than preserve the old in her memory, he would allow something grander to be built."

"It's funny how we're all influenced by our families."

He hadn't really thought of it that way until now. "You're right. But just in case you're thinking I always have a sentimental reason behind my business decisions, I would have to tell you that this is the first and only time that I've bought anything because of a personal motivation."

She smiled. "I get it. You don't want to come off weak and sappy. And I believe you rarely make decisions based on sentiment, but I'm glad that you can, because a life without emotion is really not much of a life."

He thought about that for a long while, when he wasn't thinking about how silky Isabella's hair was, how it brushed against his shoulder, how he'd love to run his hands through it and see it spread across his pillow.

When those thoughts made him shift uncomfortably in his seat, he tried to focus on the countryside, but even the dark-haired, dark-eyed children playing on the side of the road made him think of Isabella, of what her babies would look like. Would her girls have her sparkling eyes, her sense of adventure? Or would they take after him?

Damn! Another bad daydream. He'd never thought about having kids. His parents' marriage had been dismal. He'd barely spent any time with either of his parents even though he had felt the closest to his mother, but she'd always been with his dad. What was the point of bringing a child into the world if you didn't want to spend the time with them?

And he had little time in his life for anything but business.

At least, he hadn't had that time in the past.

Maybe things would be different in the future.

As Isabella had said, a life without emotion wasn't really much of a life. He knew that was true, because he'd lived that life. And he wanted more. He'd always wanted more. That was nothing new. But now that *more* included a woman…

—➤➤◀◀◀—

Argentina was a beautiful country, Isabella thought, as they passed by picturesque farms and vineyards as well as small, charming towns with lots of history. Someday she would come back and take a longer trip, explore everything the country had to offer from the dramatic glaciers to the vibrant jungle and the sprawling pampas. She owed it to herself to learn more about where she came from, not just who her father was. For too long she'd turned her back on that side of herself, and in the future that would change.

The vibration of her cell phone drew her attention. She took it out and saw her aunt's number. "It's Carlotta," she murmured.

"Take it," Nick said with a nod.

"Hola," she said.

"He came home," Carlotta said, her voice filled with emotion. "Your father came to my house this morning. He looked me in the eye, and I saw my brother for the first time in a very long time."

"Really?" she asked, shocked at the news.

"He said that last night he was visited by an angel. Her name was Isabella. She asked him to try to get better. He said he wanted to do it for her. We just took him to the clinic. He'll stay there for many weeks. Hopefully, he'll get better."

Her heart turned over in her chest as she was overwhelmed with happiness. "I'm so glad. I didn't think he recognized me or understood who I was."

"Somewhere in his head, he knew. You did this, Isabella. You brought him back."

"Do you think he'll stay at the clinic?"

"I pray that he will. He's taken the first step. Hopefully, he will continue down this path."

"Should I try to contact him again?"

"A letter would probably be appreciated, maybe a photo, give him something to look at, to care about. I'll text you the address of the clinic."

"Thank you."

"You have only yourself to thank. I'm ashamed to say I had given up."

"You don't have to be ashamed to say that. I don't know that I could have dealt with his condition for as long as you have without losing hope or the will to fight."

"We must stay in touch, Isabella, and please tell your mother how sorry I am."

"I will," she promised. She slipped the phone back into her bag and looked at Nick. "My father contacted Carlotta, and she got him to go to a clinic. He said he was visited by an angel last night."

Nick gave her a compassionate smile. "Well, he was."

"I hope he stays there and gets better. I know it's not a sure thing."

"It's a start. You got through to him, Isabella."

"I really didn't think I had, but maybe so. Or else he just thinks he had a dream. But it doesn't matter. He's in a place where he can get help. And when I return home, I'll write to him."

He put his hand on her thigh and gave it a squeeze. "You did well. You should be proud of yourself."

"Thanks." She let out a breath. "I feel so much better."

"Good." He tipped his head toward the window. "We're almost there."

She turned back to the scenery, amazed by the turquoise blue sea that sparkled under a clear blue sky and a very bright sun. "Is this your beach?"

"It's part of it," he said.

"It's beautiful, Nick."

"That three-story building is the hotel my mother wanted to visit."

"It has a sad kind of charm, but beautiful beach views. You're really going to tear it down?"

"Yes, but we'll take items from the hotel—photos, a fireplace, a window, doorknobs—and use those pieces in the resort to bring authenticity."

"It sounds like you've thought of everything." She wasn't surprised by that. Nick was nothing if not very, very thorough.

"I've been thinking about it for a long time."

As they passed by the hotel, they turned away from the beach and took a long, winding one-lane road for another few miles. The car finally stopped in front of a large three-story home with a wide veranda that wrapped around the building.

The garden in front of the house was blooming with color, and behind the home she could see a barn and some horses grazing in the more distant meadow.

An older man and a woman came out to the porch as they got out of the car. The man was short in stature with a wiry frame and an energetic stride. He had dark hair and eyes and wore a short-sleeved embroidered black shirt with gray pants. His wife was also dark, her long hair pulled back in a single braid that fell down to her waist. Almost the same height as her husband, she wore a simple peasant blouse with a long skirt. They both appeared to be in their sixties or early seventies.

"Juan and his wife, Dolores," Nick said as he helped her out of the car.

After Nick and Martin exchanged greetings with Juan and Dolores, it was her turn to accept a warm, welcoming hug from both of them.

"We are looking forward to your dance tonight," Dolores said with a smile. "We have invited our friends and family to the party."

"We're looking forward to it, too," Isabella replied, thinking it would be easier for her to say that and mean it than for Nick to do so.

"Dolores is making lunch for you. I hope you are hungry," Juan said. "After lunch, perhaps you would care for a siesta or you will have time to work, Nicholas. I know how much you like to work."

"I usually do, but I think I'd like to take a walk down to the beach before lunch—if there's time."

"Of course. There is always time. I will go with you. Would you like to join us?" Juan asked Isabella.

As much as she'd like to see the beach, she thought that Nick needed this time alone with Juan. "I'll help Dolores with lunch. You two go ahead."

"Martin?" Juan asked.

"I have to make a few more calls, so I'm going to disappear for a while as well," Martin replied.

"I'll show you your rooms," Dolores suggested. "Lunch will be ready in thirty minutes, Juan. Don't stay too long at the beach."

"We won't," Juan promised.

Isabella gave Nick an encouraging smile and then followed Dolores into the house.

———※※※———

Nick walked alongside of Juan as they took the path to the beach. They didn't speak until they reached the sand, until he was looking out at the blue-green water that had been in his dreams for so many years.

"Is it as beautiful as you remember?" Juan asked.

"My memory didn't do it justice." He looked down at Juan. "I'm glad we have a chance to speak before the party tonight."

Juan gave him a wary smile. "You are angry about my request, yes?"

"I was angry," he admitted. "We made you an extremely good offer. I think you know that."

"The land means more to me than money. I want the resort to blend with my culture and for the owner to respect the people who have lived here for hundreds of years."

"I understand that a little better now. Actually, I want to thank you, Juan. You forced me to do something I didn't want to do, and it has changed my life."

"The tango has changed your life?" Juan asked in surprise.

"Well, not exactly the tango."

Juan nodded, understanding now running through his gaze. "Ah, it is the beautiful Isabella then."

"Yes. I hired her to teach me how to dance, but she did a lot more than that. She encouraged me to look up from my work, to reconnect with my family, to stop and enjoy the small moments of life."

"That is quite a lot."

"Yes, it is." He paused. "Isabella was born in Buenos Aires. She hadn't been back here in eighteen years—until yesterday. We walked all around the city. Seeing it through her eyes made me realize how much I had missed on my last visit here. She also introduced me to some of her family members, and I enjoyed getting to know them. You were right, Juan. When I was here before, I didn't know the people. I had studied the facts, but the emotions were not important to me until someone reminded me that life without feeling is really not any kind of life." He paused. "Isabella told me that the tango is a dance of opposing desires, a battle of wills, need versus desire, love versus hate, passion versus love. The tango is a metaphor for life."

"That is very true," Juan said, his gaze thoughtful. "And you are in love with Isabella."

It wasn't a question but a statement. Still, Nick had to give an answer. "I am."

"Have you told her?"

"No."

"Why not? Are you afraid?"

He wanted to say he wasn't afraid, but the old man, with his sharp, piercing eyes, wouldn't believe that, either. "Because I don't think I've ever wanted anything or anyone as much as I want her. But she's a butterfly. I don't know if I can catch her, and even if I could catch her, is it right to keep her?"

"That is not a question I expected a cold, ruthless businessman to ask."

"I'm ruining my reputation right now."

"On the contrary," Juan said with a smile. "It's improving with every word you speak."

"Then I should tell you the rest. My mother dreamed of vacationing here in Argentina. She cut a picture out of a magazine and put it on her bulletin board fifteen years ago. When she got sick, she dreamed of getting well and going to that beach." He pulled out his wallet and the photo and passed it along to Juan. "The beach by your grandparents' hotel. Unfortunately, my mother died before that dream could come true. I want to build the resort for her. I want it to be a place where dreams are realized for thousands of people. I want it to be a special place."

"Why didn't you show me this before?" Juan asked. "Why didn't you tell me the story?"

"I didn't believe there was any room for sentiment in business. I didn't think it was important to anyone but me."

"Until I made you see that for me there is no good business unless there are strong emotions in play," Juan finished.

"Exactly."

"I will sign the contract when we get back."

He looked at Juan in surprise. "But we haven't danced yet."

"You don't need to perform for me. You have just given me the answers I was looking for. We will go back to the house, sign the contract, and toast to the creation of your beautiful new resort."

It all sounded incredibly perfect, except for one thing. "No," he said.

Juan's eyebrow lifted in shock. "No? You don't wish to buy the land?"

"I definitely want to buy the land, but I don't want you to sign the papers until after Isabella and I dance tonight. Then we'll celebrate."

Juan smiled. "I think perhaps we will have more to celebrate than just a contract."

"We'll see."

Isabella looked at herself in the mirror. She'd brought one of her most dramatically designed tango dresses with her, and it was quite simply stunning—red and black with lace and sequins. Hopefully, it would dazzle the audience, and no one would notice any small mistakes that they made in the dance.

She was a little surprised that Nick hadn't wanted to run through the dance with her before the performance, but after lunch he'd disappeared, and she'd taken a much longer nap than anticipated. Now, it was almost seven, and she could hear the chatter of the crowd downstairs.

They would dance before dinner, which she was happy about. She'd be too nervous to eat until she got Nick through the tango and hopefully through the signing of a very important contract.

A knock came at her door, and she hurried over to answer it.

Nick stood in the hallway dressed in a black tuxedo. His dark hair was slicked back, his face cleanly shaven, and there was a determined gleam in his blue eyes.

"You look beautiful," he said, his gaze filling with appreciation. "I don't know why I was worried about this dance. No one will be looking at me. All eyes will be on you."

"I doubt that. The women are certainly going to appreciate you. You're a very handsome man."

"They're ready for us downstairs."

"Are you ready?"

"As I'll ever be."

"You're going to be great, Nick. I have no doubts."

He drew in a deep breath. "I have a few doubts, but I like your confidence."

"Then it's time to dance." She gave him her hand.

He squeezed his fingers around hers. "Thank you for doing this with me."

"You're more than welcome. I'm going to make sure you get that contract."

He stared back at her as if he wanted to say something, but in the end, he leaned over and gave her a quick kiss. "For luck," he murmured.

Her lips tingled. "We don't need luck, just each other. I'll catch you if you trip, and you'll do the same for me. We'll be each other's backup."

He nodded. "I may step on your feet, but I will not let you fall, Isabella. You can trust me."

"I do. Let's go."

They walked down the stairs together and entered the living room. At least twenty people were standing around the walls of the room, the center having been cleared for their dance. The hardwood floor was slick and shiny. Isabella led Nick to the center of the floor.

Dolores was waiting to cue the music. She gave them an encouraging smile.

Isabella turned away from the crowd and faced Nick. As they took the starting position, she said, "Just look at me, Nick. There's no one else in this room. It's just you and me. I his is our dance. It doesn't have to be perfect. It just has to be honest and real."

His eyes darkened, but there was no fear in his gaze, just courage and strength and maybe a little bit of passion.

The music began. She felt as if she were about to dance the most important dance of her life. She had nothing to lose, but Nick had everything to lose, and she couldn't let that happen. She had to make sure he succeeded.

"Relax," he said.

She looked at him in astonishment. "Shouldn't I be the one saying that?"

A smile played around his lips. "You taught me well. Let me show you what I've learned."

With a murmured one-two-three, he pulled her up against his body and then she twirled away as they danced the tango better than they'd ever danced before.

Nick was amazing. Light on his feet, sure in his moves, his gaze never left hers. Stiffness had been replaced with passion, worry with desire, reluctance with enthusiasm. He wasn't thinking anymore. He was just dancing. And he was better than she'd ever imagined he could be.

The dance ended when he pulled her into his arms and then dipped her almost to the ground.

The crowd broke into applause and as he slowly pulled her back up on her feet, his gaze clung to hers. Then his mouth covered her lips, and the passion of the dance became the kiss of a lifetime. She didn't know how long it lasted, but when it was done, she was completely shaken.

There were more cheers from the audience, finally reminding both of them that they were not alone.

Juan motioned for the crowd to be quiet as he walked over to them.

"Well done," he said, appreciation in his gaze. "That was one of the best tangos I've ever seen. You found an amazing partner, Nicholas."

"I did," Nick said, looking down at her with what looked like love.

Her heart flipped over. Her pulse sped up. Was he just caught up in the moment? Or was there more going on?

"We will have a toast," Juan said as Delores handed Isabella and Nick champagne glasses. "To Nicholas Hunter, to the grand resort he will build on our land, the riches he will bring to our country, and the respect he has for our culture."

Isabella clicked her glass with Nick's and Juan's, then took a sip of the sparkling wine.

"I'd like to say something as well," Nick said. "I'm honored to build a resort here, and I won't let any of you down. This is your land, your home, and I will make sure you are pleased with everything that happens. I would also like to make a toast to Isabella, my amazing teacher and dance partner."

"Thank you," she said as they drank again.

"The buffet is now open," Juan said. "Please everyone drink, eat and enjoy yourself."

"Good job," Martin said with a happy smile. "You were fantastic, Isabella. And I never thought you could dance that well, Nick."

"I surprised myself," Nick said.

"You didn't surprise me," she told him. "I always knew you had it in you. You just had to figure that out for yourself."

"I'm going to get some food," Martin said. "Then we need to pin down Juan and get a signature on our contract."

"We will." Nick smiled at her as Martin left. "Are you hungry?"

"There's a big crowd around the table right now. I think I'll wait a bit, let my pulse slow down."

"Good idea. I want to talk to you. Come with me?"

"Okay." She set down her glass and followed him out to the patio. It was a clear, starry night, and she could see the ocean in the distance, the waves dancing through the moonbeams. "It is so beautiful here," she murmured. "You really did find paradise when you found this place."

"I'm starting to understand that it's not about the place, but about the people."

"That's true. But I'm happy for you, Nick. You danced the tango, and you got your deal."

"I already had the deal before we danced."

She was confused by his words. "What do you mean?"

"I talked to Juan earlier when we went down to the beach. I told him about my mother's dream and how learning the tango from a very wise woman changed my life. After our conversation, he told me I didn't have to dance, that he would sign the contract."

"Then why did we dance?"

"Because I wanted to dance with you. I wanted to show you that I could be a good partner—not just in the tango, but in life." He took her hands in his. "I've fallen in love with you, Isabella."

Her nerves tightened at the unexpected words. "Really, Nick? Are you sure you're not just feeling the passion of the dance?"

A smile parted his lips. "No, I've been feeling the passion for you since I first saw you. You've changed my life in a week. You're beautiful, smart, generous, insightful and have the biggest heart of anyone I've ever met. I don't know if you'd consider having a relationship with a cold, ruthless businessman, but there is one here who would like that a lot."

"You're not nearly as cold and ruthless as you make yourself out to be. And I think we're already having that relationship, as much as we've both been fighting against it." She drew in a breath, seeing a little uncertainty in his eyes and needing that to go away. "I'm in love with you, too, Nick. I need someone to push me, and you do that. I was starting to live my life in a safe, predictable way, and that wasn't going to make me happy. I went back to the theater because of you. I saw my father because of you. I also called the Tylers earlier today and told them I'd be in their show—because of you."

He smiled. "You really said yes?"

She nodded. "You made me remember who I used to be and who I want to be again. I need to let my aunt's studio go. You were right. I was using it as a place to hide out. I don't need a safe place, but I wouldn't mind a safe pair of arms."

He slid his arms around her back. "I'm more than happy to hold you, Isabella, whenever you need it."

He gazed into her eyes with so much love, she almost felt like crying. This was a man who carefully guarded his heart, but he was willing to give to her. She felt incredibly honored. "I'll do the same for you," she said, putting her arms around his neck.

"Good."

"I know that joining the theater production will make it more difficult for us to see each other."

"We'll find a way. I don't want you to give up your

dreams for me, Isabella. I want to be part of them."

"I feel the same way. You said you didn't want to be my ball and chain holding me back. I wouldn't want to do that to you, either."

He nodded in understanding. "We both have things we want to accomplish, but there are a lot of things we can do together."

She saw the wicked light in his eyes, and every nerve ending in her body started to tingle. "I like the sound of that."

"I told you before that I wasn't going to kiss you again until we could finish it."

"We're never going to finish it, Nick. Because once we start, we're going to keep going forever."

"Then let's start now."

"Finally," she said as his mouth touched hers.

She'd found love, family and home in one man, the man she would love for the rest of her life.

Epilogue

Three weeks later...

Maggie Gordon stood in the gardens of the Stratton Hotel in Napa, taking one last look at the setup for her friend Liz's wedding. A floral-covered arch would serve as the backdrop for the vows. A long white path strewn with rose petals would provide the aisle, and the two sections of white folding chairs would hopefully take care of the fifty or so guests that were now waiting in the adjoining garden for the go-ahead to take their seats for the ceremony.

She checked her watch. They were close to being on schedule, but she needed the bridesmaids together for one more wedding photo before the wedding got started.

While she loved her friends, they were notoriously difficult when it came to being ready on time and at the same time. She was sometimes part of the problem, but since the event was being held at the hotel where she worked, she was quite invested in everything going right. She knew Kate would have her head if there were any glitches. Kate might be the sweetest romantic in the group but when it came to the weddings she planned, she was a drill sergeant.

"It's beautiful," Isabella said, the first of the bridesmaids to make her way into the garden. "I love the setting. With all the tall trees surrounding us, it's like we're in a private oasis of romance and love."

Maggie smiled at the compliment. "I think so, too. I don't think Liz has seen it all set up yet. I hope she loves it."

"How could she not?"

"You look beautiful, too, Isabella."

Isabella's dark-haired, dark-eyed beauty was enhanced by the short, shimmering gold bridesmaid's dress. She didn't think the color did quite as much for her, but then she was a blue-eyed redhead with pale skin and freckles.

"You look good as well, Maggie."

"Thanks. Where's everyone else?"

"Kate is rounding them up."

"They need to hurry. The guests are in the sun right now, and it's getting warmer by the minute."

"I agree, but I think they'll get here when they get here," Isabella said with a helpless shrug. "You know how everyone is at these things."

"I'm starting to see a pattern," Maggie said dryly. "At least at Julie's wedding in a few months, I won't have the stress of making sure the location works. That will be all back in Kate's capable hands. I don't know how she does it. A wedding is so stressful. It's one day, and it has to go right."

"It will go right. The most important thing is that Liz and Michael are getting married. That's what it's all about."

"Another one bites the dust," Maggie said with a laugh. "So, is there going to be another engagement soon?" She'd heard a great deal about Isabella's new love, Nicholas Hunter, during the bridal shower and bachelorette party. She couldn't quite believe that another member of the group had fallen in love.

"Nick hasn't proposed yet. We have a lot going on right now between my show opening in a few months and his new resort opening next year, but we'll get there. I have no doubt that I am going to spend the rest of my life with that man. Who would have thought that a tango lesson would bring me my future husband?"

"Certainly not me. Soon, it's just going to be me, Jessica and Kate who are single."

"Probably not for long."

"I don't know about that. There's no one in the picture."

"You never know when that picture will change, when someone will walk into your life and sweep you off your feet. You just have to be open to the possibilities."

"I'm open, but no one has been knocking at the door."

Isabella laughed. "I'll have to see if Nick has any single friends. He is in the hotel business. You might have some friends in common."

"Nick runs hotels. I work at the front desk."

Isabella dismissed her comment with a wave of her hand. "That doesn't matter. It's not about what you do for a living; it's who you are."

That had certainly come true for Isabella, Maggie thought. A dance teacher and a hotel millionaire—definitely not the kind of combination you saw every day.

She straightened as she saw Isabella's new man walk into the garden. She could certainly see why Isabella had fallen in love. Nick Hunter was strikingly handsome.

"Hello, ladies," he said. "Where's the rest of the party?"

"Taking their sweet time," Maggie grumbled. "Thank goodness Isabella got ready on time."

He raised an eyebrow. "Really, you're on time?"

She laughed and put her arm around his waist. "I'm getting better."

An intimate look passed between them. Maggie's heart turned over at the love she saw in their eyes. She had to admit she felt both happy for Isabella and a tiny bit jealous. "I'm going to see if I can get the girls out here for a quick photo.

Don't go anywhere. I don't want to have to chase you down once I get back with the rest of the group."

"Don't worry, I'll stay here."

As Maggie left, Nick leaned in and stole a quick kiss from the beautiful woman by his side. "I thought she'd never leave," he teased.

"You're bad," she said with a laugh.

"No, I'm just addicted to you. I want you to know something, Isabella. I am going to marry you. I just don't want to rush you into anything. I want you to have time to enjoy your show and dance your heart out on the stage. But I don't want you to think that I'm afraid of commitment, because I'm not. I'm fully committed to you."

"And I to you. I'm not in a hurry, Nick. I know that I don't have the time that I want to give you right now, but—"

"But we have forever," he finished, cutting off her worried sentence. I intend to spend the rest of my life with you. We're going to have an amazing adventure together, Isabella. We're going to rule the world."

She gave him a tender loving smile. "I love how you think."

"I love everything about you." He snuck in another kiss as her friends came into the garden. "Do your thing. When you're done, I'll be here. I'll *always* be here."

Her eyes filled with moisture. "You're going to make me cry before the wedding."

"Happy tears, right?"

"So happy," she said. "I love you, Nick."

"I love you, too, Isabella."

THE END

About The Author

Barbara Freethy is a #1 New York Times Bestselling Author of 42 novels ranging from contemporary romance to romantic suspense and women's fiction. Traditionally published for many years, Barbara opened her own publishing company in 2011 and has since sold over 5 million books! Nineteen of her titles have appeared on the New York Times and USA Today Bestseller Lists.

Known for her emotional and compelling stories of love, family, mystery and romance, Barbara enjoys writing about ordinary people caught up in extraordinary adventures. Barbara's books have won numerous awards. She is a six-time finalist for the RITA for best contemporary romance from Romance Writers of America and a two-time winner for DANIEL'S GIFT and THE WAY BACK HOME.

Barbara has lived all over the state of California and currently resides in Northern California where she draws much of her inspiration from the beautiful bay area.

For a complete listing of books, as well as excerpts and contests, and to connect with Barbara:

Visit Barbara's Website:
www.barbarafreethy.com

Join Barbara on Facebook:
www.facebook.com/barbarafreethybooks

Follow Barbara on Twitter:
www.twitter.com/barbarafreethy

19252891R00121

Made in the USA
Middletown, DE
10 April 2015